SERIES

Love
ON THE EDGE

SARA MCCLAFLIN

First Edition
ISBN (trade): 979-8-9914135-5-8

Cover design: Albright Designs
Cover photography: Mykyta Starychenko and Artur Didyk
Interior format: C. Andersen
Editing: Brandy Gibson
Social Media/PA: Tawny Gratto
Marketing & PR: Wildfire Marketing Solutions

One
Ethan

THIS IS NOT WHERE I want to be.

I want to be home. Not here. I'd rather be on the couch with Cassidy, watching her pick apart a bowl of popcorn, asking me a hundred questions about the movie we've already seen twice. That's what I should be doing. That's what I always do on Saturday nights.

It's just been the two of us for a while now.

Margo, her mother, decided one day that she no longer wanted to be part of our family. Of course, it didn't start like that, hence the reason we're still legally married, hopefully not for too much longer.

She wanted to tour with her high school band. She said it was her big chance, her one shot to reclaim what she lost. I agreed, at first. Two months. I told myself I could handle two months. Cassidy and I would manage. Plus, Margo promised she'd call regularly. She promised she'd come back.

That was a year ago.

The first month, she called every other day, her voice buzzing with excitement about the road, the crowds, the freedom. By the second month, the calls became texts. Then... nothing. Just silence.

I should've seen it coming.

I replay the conversation in my head sometimes, wondering if I missed the signs.

"It's only a little while, Ethan." She stood by the door, bags lined up like soldiers, neat and ready to go. Her voice was firm, but I caught the hesitation. Just a flicker, not nearly enough to stop her.

I crossed my arms, leaning against the counter. "And Cassidy? What do I tell her when she notices you're gone?"

"Tell her I'll be back soon. Tell her I love her."

"She's seven, Margo. She's not stupid." My voice was steady, but my grip on the counter wasn't. "You think she's just going to forget you walked out with a suitcase?"

Her shoulders stiffened. No flinch. No second thoughts. Just a slow inhale, her fingers brushing through her hair, stalling. Buying time.

"She'll understand when she's older. She won't remember this."

I let out a short, bitter laugh. "She remembers everything. And when she asks me why you left, what am I supposed to say?"

That's when she looked at me—really looked at me. Hazel eyes sharp, unrelenting. Daring me to be the bad guy.

"You'll figure it out, Ethan. You always do."

It should've ended there. That was the moment I should've told her no. That she didn't get to do this. That Cassidy deserved better. But then she squared her shoulders, and her voice turned to steel.

"I've been here every single day for seven years. I gave up everything. My band, my shot, my life. Can't you give me this?"

I wanted to tell her she hadn't done it alone. That I'd been there too, holding it all together. But the weight of her guilt was too sharp, too thick to cut through.

I exhaled, rubbing a hand over my face. "How long?"

"Two months." Softer now. Hopeful, even. Like if she said it gently enough, I'd believe it.

She kissed my cheek, lingering just long enough to leave me feeling more alone than ever. Then she grabbed her bags and walked out.

The door closed with barely a sound, but it still echoed through the house.

She meant it when she said it. I think she did. But two months turned into three, then six, then twelve. She found her freedom on the road and forgot what she left behind.

Or maybe she was planning it all along. I probably should've seen it coming.

But I didn't. And Cassidy is the one paying for it.

Before I walk into Drew's, my phone buzzes.

I answer. "Hey, Ryan. What's up?" He's not only one of my closest friends, but also my attorney for the divorce I've been begging for.

"Hey. We found Margo." His voice doesn't waver, doesn't shift, doesn't offer room for hope. Just the truth.

"Where?" I let out a sigh, of relief or heartbreak, I'm not sure which.

"Halfway across the country. But the important thing is we can serve her now."

3

I have no regrets, no second thoughts, this is what we need, CC and I both need it. We have to move on and accept the fact that Margo isn't coming back.

She won't like this. But I can't find it in myself to care. I'm claiming she abandoned us because she did, there's no other way to look at it.

"You good, man?" Ryan asks when I don't respond.

"Yeah. I'm over it." I shake my head, trying to clear it from the spiral I was headed down.

"I get it. Have fun at Drew's. I'd be there if we weren't prepping for trial. Try not to worry. Let us handle everything."

"No worries. Thanks, man." It's over.

I walk into Drew's house and look around hoping to find my sister, Nina.

She told me to 'dress nice' when she demanded that I come. Whatever that means. Charcoal gray button-up, sleeves rolled up, dark jeans, boots. That'll do.

The porch is bright, lit up with strings of lights that trail into the backyard. Everything is glowing and loud.

Warm air envelopes me just as much as the music pulsing through the speakers. There's people everywhere, crowding around every space, if I wasn't as tall as I am, it'd be impossible to spot Nina in her favorite purple dress. She's laughing near the couch, like this is her stage and everyone's just here to watch.

I move toward the kitchen and grab a beer from the counter. The bar is stocked—beer, wine, liquor. Whatever you need to get through a night like this. I take a sip, let the cold settle in my chest, and lean back.

Technically this is Drew's house, but Nina's everywhere. The crystals on the bookshelf? Nina. The colorful throw blanket draped over the armchair? Nina. I've asked Drew when he's planning to propose. He just smirks. Soon, I think. It has to be soon. She's practically living here now.

Drew leans against the wall, beer in hand, watching Nina move through the crowd like she was born for this. This is all her—the lights, the music, the people—every bit of it reflects the way she throws herself into life with open arms. It's not really his thing, not the kind of night he'd plan for himself, but that doesn't matter. Because this is Nina's world, and he loves her enough to step into it without hesitation. He smirks as she pulls another friend onto the dance floor, her laughter carrying over the music. She's happy. That's what matters. So he stays, lets her do her thing, knowing she'll end up back in his arms before the night is over.

The sectional is shoved against the wall, making room for a dance floor. People are moving. Some dancing, some just swaying like the music's background noise. The glass doors to the backyard are open. I catch the flicker of a fire pit. Heated blankets are draped over chairs. Who does that? Someone needs to tell Drew that when you throw a party in winter, you use the oven, not the patio.

I drift back toward the kitchen. The counter's loaded with food—Chinese takeout, by the smell of it. Classic Drew. Cooking? Not his thing. He probably ordered all of this and then played it off like he wasn't involved.

I take another sip of my beer and lean against the counter, content to watch everyone around me.

But I'm here.

I'm here because Nina wouldn't take no for an answer.

And because... maybe I needed to be.

I decide I'll stick around for a little while. Grab a drink, make an appearance, then head out. Maybe I'll pick Cassidy up early from my mom's. She's supposed to stay the night, but I keep checking my phone just in case.

Before I can take another sip of my beer, it happens. Fast. Too fast to react.

A blur of movement. Someone trips. And suddenly, something cold and wet is soaking through my shirt.

I freeze. Look down and see a dark cocktail dripping down my chest.

The culprit—a woman with wide, mortified eyes—stares up at me like she just spilled on a tiger. And for a second, I forget about the mess. She is beautiful. Dark hair in a braid, sharp cheekbones, deep brown eyes that flick between panic and something else. I don't know what that is, yet.

"Oh my God. I'm so sorry! I didn't see you there," she blurts, words tumbling over each other.

She snatches a cocktail napkin from a nearby table and starts dabbing at my shirt. It's doing absolutely nothing, but her frantic effort is... something.

I raise an eyebrow, holding back a smirk. "Well, that's one way to make an introduction."

She freezes mid-dab, then lets out an apologetic laugh. "First impressions are my specialty. Clearly."

I shake my head, chuckling. "Could've been worse. At least it's not beer."

"Small mercies," she mutters, the corners of her lips curving up slightly. She finally gives up on the napkin, crumpling it in her hand. "I swear I'm not usually this clumsy."

"Right," I say, amused. "This is just a one-time thing?"

"Exactly." She nods. "You just had the bad luck of being my victim."

She holds out her hand, confidence creeping back in. "I'm Valeria, by the way."

I take it. My grip firm, but easy.

"Ethan." For some reason, I don't let go right away. "Nice to meet you, Valeria."

I watch as she leans against the wall next to me, just outside the chaos of the party. I thought she'd laugh off the spill, make a joke, and disappear back into the crowd. But she doesn't. She stays.

I take a sip of my beer, glancing at her. "Not heading back into the action?"

She tilts her head, smirk easy but knowing. "Definitely not my scene."

I raise an eyebrow. "So the drink-spilling thing... that wasn't just part of your big plan to blend in?"

She laughs, soft but genuine, shaking her head. "No, but if it was, I'd say it worked out. No one's staring at me, so that's a win."

Her response surprises me. No awkward apology, no fake charm. Just honesty.

"So, what are you doing here?" I ask, leaning back against the wall beside her.

She sighs, brushing her hair out of her face. "A friend dragged me here. Said I needed to 'get out of my comfort zone.'" She glances at the crowd. "Apparently, my life is boring."

I chuckle, tipping my beer toward her. "Join the club. My sister's responsible for this. She thinks I need to 'socialize.'"

She laughs. "So this is her idea of you cutting loose?"

"Apparently," I smirk. "Though I don't think standing here with a beer and a wet shirt was part of the plan."

Her laugh lingers this time, warm and unguarded. "Maybe we're both bad at this party thing."

"Maybe," I agree, letting the word settle between us.

The party hums in the background, distant now, even though we're still in the middle of it. She doesn't seem in a hurry to move.

"You're really not heading back in?" I tease.

She smirks. "Do I look like I belong out there?"

I glance at the crowd, then back at her. "No. You don't."

She raises an eyebrow. "Wow. Thanks."

I chuckle, shaking my head. "I mean that in a good way. You stand out."

Her expression softens. She leans back against the wall, shoulder brushing against it. "No, you're right." A pause. Then she tilts her head at me.

Her lips twitch like she's considering something. Then she gives me a playful look. "Then what are you still doing here?"

"Good question." I watch her as the party noise blurs into the background. "Maybe I was meant to run into you."

Her gaze holds mine a second longer before she smirks. "Well then," she says, voice teasing but curious. "If you were meant to run into me, what's the plan now? Enlighten me."

I chuckle, tilting my beer toward her. "Enlighten you? That might take some time. You in a rush?"

She shrugs, eyes flicking toward the crowd before settling back on me. "Not anymore."

She laughs, tucking her hair behind her ear. "Guilty. I'm more of a keep my head down and stay focused kind of person."

"Focused on what?" I ask, actually curious now.

She hesitates, just for a second. "Work. Goals. You know, boring stuff."

I raise an eyebrow. "What kind of goals?"

Her lips twitch like she's debating how much to say. "Big ones."

"Big ones?" I press, smiling. "That's vague. Like, saving-the-world big, or personal-world-domination big?"

She laughs, shaking her head. "Somewhere in between. Let's just say I don't leave a lot of room for... distractions."

I glance at the crowd, then back at her. "This doesn't seem like the kind of place for someone avoiding distractions."

"Exactly," she replies, tone wry. "Like I said, my friend dragged me here. She's convinced I need to have some semblance of a life outside of work."

"Do you?" I ask.

"Do I what?"

"Need to have some semblance of a life?"

She hesitates, gaze flicking to her drink. "I don't know," she admits quietly. "Maybe."

The honesty in her answer surprises me, and I find myself watching her more closely. She taps her fingers lightly against her cup, her mind clearly working through something.

"What about you?" she asks suddenly, shifting the attention back to me. "What's your excuse for being here if this isn't your thing either?"

I shrug, leaning back against the wall. "Same reason, I guess. My sister thinks I need to 'socialize.'"

"And?" she presses, tilting her head. "Is it working?"

I glance around the room before looking back at her, smirking. "You're standing here talking to me, so I'd say it's working."

She lets out a short laugh, shaking her head. "Good save."

"Who says I'm saving anything?" I hold her gaze.

Her lips part slightly like she's about to respond, then she just shakes her head, a small laugh escaping. It's small, but I can't look away, I'm completely captivated by the dark red of lips.

We stand in silence a little longer, the buzz of the party fading as I glance at her. She doesn't seem in a rush to go back.

"So, Ethan," she says suddenly, tilting her head. "If parties aren't your thing, what is?"

I smirk, taking a sip of my beer. "That's a loaded question."

She raises an eyebrow. "Alright, let me narrow it down. What do you like to do when you're not... here?"

I chuckle. "Work, mostly. I spend a lot of time at the garage."

She tilts her head. "Garage?"

I nod. "I work on cars. Repairs, restorations, maintenance—you name it."

Her eyes light up slightly, curiosity sparking. "So, you're a car guy?"

"Guess so," I shrug. "I like figuring out how things work. Cars just... make sense. Every part has a purpose. If something's broken, you fix it."

She leans against the wall, the slit in her dress exposing her thigh. "That's a good way to look at it. So, it's not just a job for you?"

"Not really," I admit. "I like it. The hands-on work, the problem-solving. It's... satisfying."

Her expression softens slightly. "Must be nice, working with something you actually like. Not everyone gets to do that."

"Yeah," I say, nodding. "It is. Not glamorous or anything, but it's good, honest work."

I take another sip of my beer, watching as she leans comfortably against the wall, away from the chaos of the party. She doesn't look bored. She looks... entertained. Like she's enjoying making me work for this conversation.

I tip my beer toward her. "Alright, my turn."

She smirks. "Your turn for what?"

"For questions." I nod at her. "I told you what I do. What about you?"

She tilts her head, considering, then shrugs. "I work."

I let out a short laugh. "Wow. Great answer. Really deep."

Her lips twitch. "I like to keep things mysterious."

I shake my head. "Alright, fine. Let's play a game. I'll guess, and you tell me if I'm warm or cold."

She sighs, exaggerated, like this is a hassle. "Fine. But if you say accountant, I'm walking away."

I smirk. "Noted. You don't seem like the type to sit behind a desk all day."

She lifts her cup in a toast. "Warm."

"Something physical. Personal trainer?"

She scrunches her nose. "Cool."

"Yoga instructor?"

Her laughter spills out before she can stop it. "Ice cold."

I narrow my eyes. "Lumberjack?"

She raises an eyebrow. "Do I look like I cut down trees for a living?"

I shrug. "I don't know, you've got strong arms."

She snorts, shaking her head. "You're ridiculous."

"But warm, right?"

She rolls her eyes. "Fine. Warm."

I lean in slightly. "So... you're obviously some kind of athlete."

She takes a slow sip of her drink before answering. "Warmer."

I point my beer at her. "Aha. I knew it. You give off that whole 'wake up at 5 AM and train until you hate yourself' vibe."

She exhales a dramatic sigh. "Busted."

I grin. "Okay, final guess. You're a professional dodgeball player."

She bursts out laughing, and I swear it's one of the sweetest sounds I've ever heard. "Yeah, you got me. Nationally ranked."

I shake my head. "I knew it."

She smirks, but there's something flickering behind it—like she's enjoying this but still holding something back.

I arch a brow. "You love it?"

She hesitates a second too long before nodding. "Yeah. I do."

I watch her, amused. "And yet, you won't actually tell me what you do."

She grins. "Nope."

I chuckle, shaking my head. "So I tell you I work with cars, and you make me play '20 Questions' to find out what you do?"

"Sounds fair to me," she says, smirking.

I take another sip of my beer, considering her. She's interesting. Not just because she won't answer, but because she enjoys the game.

I tilt my beer slightly in her direction. "You're something else."

She lifts her drink. "So I've been told."

The music changes, the bass kicks harder, the beat heavier. A couple stumbles past, tripping over each other. I have no idea if they just met or if they're actually together, but she spills her drink on the way, so I know they're drunk.

"That's my cue," Valeria says.

I glance at her. She's watching them too.

"Done already?" I ask, chuckling.

"I think I hit my limit about ten minutes ago," she says, eyes flicking toward the crowd. "I don't even know half these people. And the ones I do? I'd rather not."

"Do you need an escape plan?" I ask, smirking.

She looks at me, and I laugh harder.

"You offering one?" she asks.

She's quick-witted. I like that about her.

"I've got a truck outside and a solid track record of avoiding bad situations. Seems like a good deal."

She pretends to think it over. "Hmm. So what's the catch?"

"No catch," I say, shrugging. "Just two people ditching a party they didn't want to be at in the first place."

She looks around, still thinking. Probably about how bad of an idea it is to leave with a total stranger.

Finally, she finishes the last sip of her drink. "Alright. Let's go before my friend finds me and gives me another speech about 'loosening up.'"

"You spilled a drink on a stranger. That's got to count for something."

She nudges me playfully, as we push off the wall and head for the door.

The cool night air is a sharp contrast to the heat inside. Valeria pulls her jacket tighter around her.

I unlock the truck and glance at her. "Regretting your decision already?"

"Not yet," she teases, sliding into the passenger seat. "But let's see where this night takes us first."

I smirk, closing the driver's side door. "Guess we will."

I slide into the driver's seat and turn to her. "So, where are we going?"

"I would say home, but I don't need my parents asking me how the party went and why I'm home so early," she says.

"Oh, I feel that," I say.

She exhales, like she's debating whether to say more. "I'm trying to move out, but honestly, my parents aren't home enough for me to warrant it."

She looks away, almost embarrassed.

"You don't owe me an explanation," I say, keeping my voice even. "I get it. No judgment."

She nods, then shifts in her seat. "How about we go somewhere quiet? Hang out for a bit?"

"Deal," I say, putting the truck in drive.

I know the perfect spot. A clearing not far from Drew's house. People use it for stargazing, but this late, it'll be empty. Quiet. A good place to breathe.

Two
Valeria

I'M SO GLAD I left the party.

But leaving with this guy? Definitely not part of the plan.

We sit in silence, but there's no awkwardness. I like that. No pressure to talk. No need to fill the quiet with meaningless words. I've never been good at it, hence why my sport of choice isn't a team sport.

I have no idea where we're going. Just that Ethan knows a spot.

I keep peeking over at him. I tell myself I'm just checking where we are, but that's a lie.

The glow from the dashboard catches on the sharp angles of his face—strong jaw, lips slightly parted, focused on the road like nothing can shake him. His hands grip the wheel, fingers steady, forearms tense just enough to make me wonder how it would feel if he ever let go.

He's hot. Effortlessly, unfairly hot. The kind of guy who probably looks good without even trying. Broad shoulders, strong arms, the kind of build that comes from real work, not just lifting weights in a gym. Sandy blond hair that's just a little too messy, like he ran a hand through it without thinking. And those eyes—blue, sharp, watching me like he's already trying to figure me out.

And the worst part? I don't think he even knows it.

We pull up to the spot. A wide-open field, dark except for the sky above us. Out here, the stars feel closer, endless, stretching beyond anything I can explain. The air is crisp, cool against my skin. The quiet settles in, wrapping around us like a second blanket. It's peaceful.

Too peaceful.

"Do you want to sit in the bed of the truck for a bit?" Ethan asks.

I nod. "Sure."

He lowers the tailgate and spreads out a blanket. I hop up the best I can, adjusting my dress as I settle in. The metal beneath me is cold, but I barely feel it. I lean back, tilting my head up.

"Wow," I breathe. "It's beautiful here."

Ethan climbs in beside me, another blanket in hand. He spreads it over us, the weight of it pressing lightly against my legs, adding warmth to the air between us.

"You came prepared," I say, glancing at him.

He smirks but doesn't answer.

I settle into the silence, eyes tracing the sky. The stars are sharper, scattered like someone spilled diamonds across the darkness. I don't know why, but I expected them to look different out here. Closer, maybe.

"I just realized I have no idea what I'm looking at," I admit.

"Me either." Ethan shifts slightly beside me. "It's just nice to look at something that's unexplainable."

The quiet stretches, long enough that I shift beneath the blanket. Not uncomfortable, just thick. Charged, like we're both waiting for something to break it.

I glance at him. He's leaning back, legs stretched out, arms resting loosely at his sides. Like this is just another night.

But it doesn't feel like just another night.

The silence sits heavier now. I feel it in my chest, pressing down, making my breath feel shallow. I tell myself it's nothing, but I still shift slightly, my fingers toying with the edge of the blanket, my body tense in a way I don't understand.

I glance at Ethan again, just for a second. But this time, he's already looking at me.

His smirk fades, just slightly. No longer playful, more assessing.

Something low in my stomach tightens, heat unfurling slow and unshakable, pooling beneath my skin. I lick my lips, glancing away.

I need to break the silence.

"You sure you're not some secret astronomy nerd?" I nudge him lightly with my elbow. "Because that was deep."

Ethan grins but doesn't look at me. "I have my moments."

I roll my eyes, turning toward him. "Not even the North Star?"

"Vaguely familiar," he says, voice low, amused.

"Cassiopeia?"

"Sounds like a fancy cocktail."

I scoff. "Wow. You are truly hopeless."

"I never claimed otherwise." He finally turns, looking at me now. His gaze is steady, unreadable. Something about it makes my breath catch for half a second.

I arch an eyebrow, playing it off. "And here I thought you had layers."

"Oh, I do." His smirk deepens. "You just haven't peeled them back yet."

Heat spreads through me, quick and uninvited. My pulse jumps, my breath hitching slightly before I force it steady.

I lick my lips, suddenly too aware of the way he's watching me. The teasing has shifted. The air is different, warmer.

"You keep looking at me," Ethan says, his voice lower now. Almost lazy.

I shrug, tilting my chin up. "Maybe I like what I see."

His smirk lingers, but his eyes drop slightly—like he's just noticing something he hadn't before.

The night isn't peaceful anymore. It's different. I don't want to fight it. I don't think I could if I tried.

Without giving myself the chance to back out or talk myself out of it, I lean in and kiss Ethan.

It's supposed to be just a test, just curiosity. But the second our lips touch, everything shifts. I pull back, breathless, but Ethan doesn't let me go. His hand slides behind my neck, fingers threading into my hair, pulling me back in. This kiss is different, deeper. There's no hesitation or second guessing.

Something tight unravels inside me.

The teasing, the tension—we've been circling this moment all night. And now that we're here, it crashes into me, fast, urgent, impossible to ignore.

The blanket slips off my shoulders as Ethan moves, his hands sliding down to my thighs. He grips my waist, pulling me closer, pressing me back against the truck bed.

His mouth trails along my jaw, his breath hot against my skin. My pulse pounds beneath his lips.

I don't think. I just feel.

His body, his hands, the way he fits between my legs as I straddle him. Heat settles low in my stomach, thick and pulsing.

His name leaves my lips in a shaky breath, and that's all it takes.

It's the way his touch burns through me, the way my body reacts before my mind can catch up.

Ethan notices. He reads it instantly.

He stills, his fingers barely there against the lace of my underwear, his breath warm against my jaw.

"Tell me if you want me to stop."

His voice is rough, thick with restraint. His hands don't move away, but he pulls back slightly. Waiting.

I don't want space.

I don't want him to wait.

I grab his wrist, not to push him away—but to make sure he doesn't let go.

His exhale is sharp and controlled, while his blue gaze stays locked on mine. His fingers flex under my grip before they slide higher, teasing, testing, tracing slow patterns along my inner thigh.

My breath falters.

I arch into him, my legs parting before I can think twice. I shouldn't want this as badly as I do, I don't even know his last name.

Ethan must feel the way I tremble because his lips brush against my ear, slow and deliberate.

"I've got you, Val." His voice is deeper now, something dark curling around the edges, something I feel everywhere.

Then he moves, his fingers slipping beneath the lace, and I stop thinking altogether.

Ethan's fingers brush against bare heat, and my whole body tenses. It's instinct, a shock at the intimacy of it, but it's not hesitation. It's need.

He groans softly, his breath warm against my cheek as he moves again, fingertips gliding through the slickness pooling between my thighs.

"You're already so wet for me," he rasps, his voice low, thick, like he's barely holding himself back. His fingers stroke deeper, slow and deliberate, sliding between my folds before circling my clit in a featherlight touch that has my breath catching in my throat.

I gasp, back arching as heat pulses low in my stomach. My hips jerk slightly, chasing the sensation, and Ethan chuckles, the sound dark and knowing.

"Right there?" His tone is teasing, but there's an edge to it, like he's memorizing every reaction.

I grip his shoulders, nodding because I can't find words, not when he keeps moving, pressing deeper, rubbing slow, torturous circles against my most sensitive spot. The pleasure is sharp, consuming, something I can't hold back.

"Relax, Val," he murmurs, his free hand sliding up my side, fingers pressing into my ribs just enough to ground me. His lips graze my ear, sending another shiver down my spine. "I've got you."

Then he moves lower, his fingers testing, stretching, slipping just inside, and my breath stutters, a moan breaking free before I can stop it.

Ethan stills, waiting, watching me.

I don't pull away.

I don't want him to stop.

I roll my hips, pressing into his touch, and that's all it takes.

He curses softly, then moves again, filling me little by little, his fingers stroking, coaxing, learning me with every slow, careful movement.

And I come undone for him, right there, beneath the stars.

I can still feel the aftershocks pulsing through me, my body twitching as the last waves of pleasure fade into something warmer, heavier. My skin feels too hot, my breath unsteady, my legs still weak around his waist.

I should let the silence sit. Let him move. Let him take everything.

Instead, I open my mouth. "Before we go any further, I want to talk about this."

I shouldn't. But I do.

Ethan tenses slightly, pulling back just enough to look at me. "About what?"

He's still above me, still holding himself up, but I know—if I tell him to stop, he will.

I swallow hard, licking my lips. "I don't have time for anything other than one night. That's all this can be," I say, rushed, like if I don't get it out fast enough, I won't say it at all.

His smirk fades, just slightly. He studies me for a second, gaze unreadable, before his lips part. "One night?"

"One night," I say again, firmer this time.

He watches me for a second longer, like he's considering something, before the smirk returns—slow, knowing. "I can do that."

Then his mouth is on mine again, kissing me deep, pulling me back into the heat, into the moment, into exactly where I want to be.

I hesitate. Just for a second. Then I push the thought away.

I decide not to tell him. He doesn't need to know this is my first time. Because he'll stop. He'll hesitate.

And I don't want him to. I want to keep going.

I watch as he shifts, his breath uneven, fingers moving to his belt. The soft clink of metal fills the quiet space between us, followed by the slow, deliberate sound of his zipper lowering.

My pulse hammers, heat rushing to my face, my throat tightening.

Ethan keeps his eyes on me, watching my reaction as he reaches into his back pocket. A small foil packet catches the faint glow of the stars.

He tears it open with his teeth, and my stomach clenches at the effortless movement, the quiet confidence in the way he handles it.

But when he pushes his jeans down just enough and wraps his hand around himself, I stop thinking altogether.

My breath catches, my thighs pressing together instinctively before he settles between them again, his body warm and solid against mine.

Ethan leans in, his mouth brushing against my ear, his voice rough with restraint.

"You good?" Ethan murmurs, voice low, eyes locked on mine.

I nod, maybe too fast. "Yeah. I'm good."

His smirk deepens, like he doesn't quite believe me, but he doesn't call me out on it.

"Yeah?" His fingers skim down my thigh, teasing, testing, as he leans in. "Prove it."

The challenge in his voice ignites something in me, something reckless.

I pull him down into a kiss, hard and desperate, trying to match the fire burning through me.

But Ethan takes control, his hand gripping my hip, his body pressing into mine, making me feel just how badly I've already lost.

He presses closer, his weight settling between my thighs, his body hot and heavy against mine. His breath is warm against my neck, his fingers gripping my hips as if to steady himself—or maybe to steady me.

I feel him right there, the tip of his length brushing against my entrance, teasing, testing. My entire body tenses in anticipation, a shiver racing down my spine.

He moves slowly, carefully, pressing forward just an inch, and my breath catches. The pressure is sharp, unfamiliar, foreign. My body instinctively clenches around him, resisting, unsure.

Ethan groans, his forehead pressing to mine, his fingers tightening on my waist.

He presses a lingering kiss to my jaw, his breath warm against my skin. "Relax, Val. Let me in." His voice is deep, rough, coaxing—not questioning, just guiding.

I exhale shakily, forcing myself to relax. I want this. I want him. But my body is still learning, still adjusting to something it's never felt before.

He moves again—just a little deeper. The stretch burns, a slow, aching pull that makes me gasp, my nails digging into his shoulders.

Then everything stops.

Ethan freezes.

Completely.

His muscles lock, his breathing sharp and uneven, his fingers flexing against my hips like he's trying to process something he wasn't expecting.

His forehead tilts against mine, voice strained. "Val... shit."

He doesn't move. His grip on my hips tightens, his muscles locking up. Something shifts between us. I don't know if it's the way I fit against him or the way his breath catches, but I feel it—he does too.

I shift beneath him, rolling my hips, trying to take him deeper, trying to pull him back into the urgency we had seconds ago. The ache is sharp, stretching, but there's something else creeping in beneath it—something hotter, heavier, twisting low in my stomach.

Ethan doesn't let me.

His hands clamp down, holding me still. "You should've told me." His voice is rough, almost like a growl, not soft, not careful. Just frustrated.

I bite my lip, fingers digging into his arms, urging him on. "Well, there's no time like the present."

He exhales sharply, shaking his head, jaw clenched. "This isn't something you just do with someone you barely know."

I tighten my legs, pulling him closer, deeper. "I want this, Ethan. And I don't waste time wanting things I don't plan to have."

I rock my hips, forcing more of him inside me, welcoming the sting, the overwhelming fullness, the way my body stretches to take him.

Ethan swears under his breath, his fingers twitching, his control slipping.

I drag my hands up his back, my nails pressing into his skin. "You stopping now?" My voice comes out breathy, taunting. "Or are you gonna fuck me like you were about to?"

His breath falters. His restraint cracks.

He mutters another curse, his grip tightening as he finally pushes in deeper, burying himself inside me completely. The stretch burns, and I gasp, my back arching beneath him, the pain twisting with something else—something raw and consuming.

Ethan groans low in his throat, head dipping to my shoulder. "You're fucking reckless."

"So are you," I breathe, rolling my hips against him.

His fingers flex on my thighs, and then he pulls back just enough to slam into me again, dragging a choked moan from my lips.

"You're gonna feel me for days," he mutters, voice thick, breath ragged.

I can't wait.

Ethan's pace stays steady, his grip firm as he moves inside me. My body is still trembling, oversensitive from release, but the heat doesn't fade. It lingers, spreading slow and thick, something unfamiliar and all-consuming.

The pressure builds, sharp and unbearable, my breath coming in ragged, uneven gasps. My nails dig into his back, my thighs trembling around his waist, the sensation pushing me toward something I don't understand.

Ethan must feel it—the way I clench around him, the way I arch into his touch, the way my body begs for something I've never had before.

"That's it," he rasps, voice rough, his mouth skimming my jaw. "Let it happen."

I don't know how.

The tension keeps winding tighter, hotter, so sharp it almost aches—

And then it snaps.

A cry breaks from my lips as pleasure crashes through me, shattering everything in its path. Heat surges through my veins, so intense it leaves me shaking beneath him. My body clenches hard around his, waves of sensation rolling through me, endless, unstoppable.

Ethan groans, deep and guttural, his grip tightening as he thrusts into me harder, faster, his restraint slipping away. His breath stutters, rough and uneven, his muscles going rigid.

I feel it—the second he loses control.

A curse spills from his lips as his rhythm stutters, his forehead pressing against mine, his entire body tensing before he buries himself deep, groaning as he lets go.

The truck bed is hard beneath us, but neither of us notice.

There's only the aftershocks pulsing through me, the way my body still trembles against his, the way my heart won't slow down.

I don't know what happens next.

I just know I don't want to move.

Three

Valeria

I WAKE UP SORE. The ache is dull, nothing unexpected, but it lingers. A reminder.

I shift beneath the sheets, and the memories slip in before I can stop them.

"We should go," Ethan says, voice even, unreadable. Not distant. Just matter-of-fact.

I stare up at the sky for a second longer, my body still warm, my skin still tingling, every muscle loose in a way I've never felt before. The stars look the same, but something in me feels different. Not changed—just... lighter.

"Yeah." I push myself up, smoothing my dress back down my thighs. Ethan shifts beside me, zipping his jeans, running a hand through his hair. He's half-dressed, still a little breathless, but not in a hurry.

No awkwardness. No hesitation.

This is just one night. And that's exactly how I want it.

Ethan stands first, reaching for the tailgate before pausing, looking at me like he's checking for something. Trying to see if I regret what we did

"You good?"

I pull my jacket around me, nodding. "Yeah. You?"

"Yeah." A small smirk, barely there, before he hops down from the truck bed and reaches for his keys. Like this is nothing new to him. Like this is exactly what it was supposed to be.

I follow him into the cab, settling into the passenger seat as he starts the engine. The truck rumbles to life, the headlights cutting through the dark, the quiet settling in around us.

We don't talk as he drives. Not because it's weird. Not because there's something to say.

Because there isn't. Because this is exactly what I wanted.

And yet, for some reason, I don't look at him. And he doesn't look at me.

I can't just lay here all day. I need to get up. I need to get ready.

Practice starts at 5 AM. It's already 4:30.

I go straight to the bathroom and brush out my hair. When I look in the mirror, something feels off. I look... happy? Maybe. Lighter. Looser.

I tie my hair into a bun and splash cold water on my face. I need to focus. It was just one night. It doesn't change anything. It can't.

Today is a technique clinic. Jumps and spins. Something about them feels wrong lately, and I don't have time for anything to be anything but perfect. I need to fix it. I need to get to work.

I ARRIVE AT THE rink just before we're supposed to step on the ice.

The cold air wraps around me the second I push through the doors, crisp and sharp, laced with the familiar scent of ice, rubber mats, and the faint metallic bite of skate blades waiting to be used. The overhead lights buzz softly, casting bright reflections across the untouched surface of the rink.

Harry Benson, one of the owners, is on the Zamboni, guiding it in slow, steady laps across the ice. He's been doing this for decades—late sixties now, but still as steady as ever. I wave as I pass. Joanne, his wife, is in the office, unlocking doors, switching on lights, bringing the rink to life the way she has every morning for the last thirty years. They've owned this place forever, and it shows in the way they move, like the rink is as much a part of them as they are of it.

"Good morning, honey," she calls, her voice is warm and familiar.

"Good morning, Jo," I reply.

"Ready for practice?"

"Ready as I'll ever be."

She laughs as I head to the locker room, her voice trailing behind me as I push through the door.

The room is stark. Metal lockers line the walls, paint slightly worn from years of use, a few dented from careless kicks or slammed doors. The overhead lights are bright but harsh, casting sharp reflections off the smooth tile floor.

A row of benches sits in the center, scratched and scuffed from skates being tossed down carelessly. Along the far wall, there's a bathroom with a couple of stalls and a row of sinks beneath a long mirror, its edges slightly fogged from years of humidity. The faint scent of disinfectant lingers in the air, mixed with something colder—rubber, ice, the familiar bite of the rink settling into every surface.

Nothing much to it. Just a space to change, lace up, and get to work.

I drop my bag onto the bench. The sound echoes in the empty room.

I grab my skates from my locker and take a seat. The repetitive motion of lacing up my skates is comforting. It's the kind of thing I can do without thinking, the monotony of it giving me a brief break from everything else. Muscle memory. Habit. Routine.

I hear someone plop down next to me, the bench jolting slightly from the impact. I don't need to look up—I already know who it is. No one else moves like that, all energy and ease, like the world is hers to take up space in. Like she belongs everywhere, including right here, right now, beside me.

Nina. "Hey, Val!" she says, grinning. She's quick with her skates, hands moving efficiently like she's already eager to get on the ice.

"Hey. Ready to skate?" I finish the last lace, tightening it just right before giving her a smile of my own. Despite the late night, I'm feeling more energized than I have in a while, it's... refreshing.

"Always am!" She leans back slightly, stretching her arms. "So, I volunteered to help coach the beginner classes. Harry and Jo have so many sign-ups they had to add more classes. Think you can help?"

I pause, fingers tightening around my skate lace. Coaching? Kids? Not exactly my thing. I know I can help, but do I want to? Not really. I don't have the patience. I don't have the interest. I don't even know if I have the ability. Some skaters love coaching, they love passing on what they know, love seeing the next generation improve under their guidance. That's not me.

"I don't think so, Nina. I'm not the coaching type."

She just shrugs. "Well, if you change your mind, I can always use the help."

That's one of the things I love about Nina. She doesn't push. She just lets me be. No judgment, no disappointment, just an open door if I ever decide to walk through it. Except of course, convincing me to go to that party last night.

Nina tilts her head slightly, her voice shifting, softening. "I didn't see you last night. Did you come?"

I freeze for half a second—just half a second—but it's enough. Heat creeps into my cheeks before I can stop it. I don't look at her. I look at my skates instead, pretending I'm focused on adjusting them, like I need to buy myself a few extra seconds to answer.

"I did," I say, forcing casual into my voice. "But I left probably earlier than most."

Nina's eyes narrow just slightly. "What? With who?"

My stomach clenches.

I could lie. I could change the subject, make a joke, deflect. But lying to Nina never works.

"Just a guy who drove me home," I say quickly. Too quickly. Too light.

35

She doesn't miss a beat. Her eyebrows lift, and I swear I can hear her suppressing a laugh. "A guy?"

I laugh too, but it's forced, awkward. "It's not that big of a deal."

It is. Or at least, it feels like it is.

Because I don't do this. This isn't me. And the fact that I'm even dodging Nina's questions, the fact that I'm acting like this is something I need to downplay? That's not me either.

But I don't want to tell her.

I don't want to tell her what I did with a stranger. How reckless it was. How out of character it was.

I don't regret it. That's not the problem.

The problem is that it should have been simple. A one-night thing. No complications. No second thoughts. No lingering weight pressing against my ribs, making me feel like I stepped into something I don't fully understand yet.

I don't want to explain that to Nina. I don't even want to explain it to myself.

So I don't. I let the silence sit between us for a second too long before I force out a response.

"I'll share it with you one day... maybe."

Even as I say it, I know I won't. Not anytime soon.

Nina just laughs, shakes her head. "Alright, keep your secrets."

She doesn't press. She knows I'll talk when I'm ready. If I'm ever ready.

"Come on, ladies! We don't have all day!" a voice calls from outside the locker room.

"Let's go, Val. Time to practice," Nina says.

We get up and head for the door. The chill hits us immediately, but I'm used to it by now. Technical training day. The one day every skater dreads.

Our coach, Nikolai Petrov, is a drill master. He trains the top three skaters and helps run the skating school program. He doesn't take it easy on anyone. We all know what we're in for.

Nina and I step onto the ice, and I spot Zara Hart in the corner stretching. While Nina started skating later, Zara and I have been skating since we were kids. We grew up pushing each other, constantly fighting to be the best.

Zara is petite but powerful, built for precision and speed. Her jet-black hair is pulled into a sleek ponytail, her striking green eyes locked in quiet focus as she leans into a deep stretch, one foot pressed against the boards. Even now, just warming up, she looks composed, deliberate, like she's already calculating every movement before stepping onto the ice.

She's wearing a fitted black athletic jacket over a bold-patterned leotard—bright colors, sharp lines, a perfect match for the way she skates. Her leggings hug the lean muscle in her legs, strength carved from years of training. Zara doesn't waste energy on unnecessary chatter, not when there's work to be done.

She lifts her head slightly, noticing us, and gives a small nod before adjusting her position. That's all. No words. Just acknowledgement.

I roll my shoulders and push off the boards hard, legs burning as I dig deep into my crossovers. My strides are long, deliberate, every push slicing into the ice with force. The wind rushes against my face as I gather speed, but it's not enough.

"Faster!" Nikolai's voice cuts through the rink like a blade, sharp and commanding.

I don't hesitate. I drive forward, crossovers crisp, each push more powerful than the last. My skates cut deep into the ice, carving it with precision. I don't need to look to know that I'm ahead. I can hear Nina and Zara behind me, their blades slashing against the ice, pushing to keep up.

We reach the boards. I pivot sharply, my body moving without thought, and launch into another sprint. I don't feel the burn in my legs anymore—just the rhythm, the control, the sheer momentum that carries me forward.

"Good," Nikolai calls as I hit the opposite boards first. "Again."

I reset, push off hard, faster this time. Nina is keeping pace now, but I force myself to dig deeper, to go faster. I hit the final crossover and stop abruptly, ice spraying at my feet.

"That is what I want," Nikolai says, his gaze locked on me before flicking to the others. "The rest of you, push harder. Valeria should not be this far ahead."

I glance at Nina and Zara, breathing hard, but they don't look annoyed—just determined.

"Show-off," Nina mutters under her breath, but there's a grin on her face.

"Not my fault," I shrug, smirking back at her. "Try harder." She nudges me with her elbow before skating toward center ice.

"Edge drills," Nikolai commands. "Control. Depth. No wasted movement."

I drop into my edges, carving deep, my body shifting effortlessly between inside and outside edges. My weight stays perfectly centered, my movements fluid. Nikolai watches me closely, but for once, he says nothing.

I know what that means. Approval.

I glance over at Nina and Zara, both strong skaters, but I know my technique is cleaner. My control is sharper. My foundation has always been my greatest strength.

"Stronger knees," Nikolai calls, but it's not directed at me. Zara adjusts her form. Nina grits her teeth and deepens her edge.

We move into turns, flowing through three-turns, rockers, counters. I barely think as I move, letting muscle memory take over. This is where I thrive— technical, clean. Every movement is intentional.

"Jumps," Nikolai calls next.

I reset, launching into a loop jump, my blade biting into the ice as I land cleanly. I barely have to check my exit before transitioning into another, then another.

Nina lands hers with ease. Zara's is strong but slightly tilted forward on the landing.

I step into a flip jump, my arms tight, my rotation fast, my landing solid. Then a lutz—deep edge, explosive height, clean check-out. I feel Nikolai watching, analyzing, waiting for something to correct. But there's nothing.

"Axels," he calls.

I already know the drill. Takeoff, arms tight, fast rotation, land strong.

I go first. I launch into my double axel, air position locked, rotation perfect. The ice meets my blade perfectly, my landing silent, my exit controlled.

"Excellent," Nikolai says. "Again."

I don't hesitate. I push off again, stronger, faster.

"Triple Toe?" Nina teases.

I smirk. "Watch me."

This time I land with a slight wobble, but nothing that would cost me in competition.

Nikolai nods. "Good. Spins."

Nikolai calls out the next drill, and I move into a spin. They're clean, controlled, exactly how they should be.

But something about it feels hollow.

The technique is there, the execution solid, but it's just that—execution. A sequence of perfected movements without anything behind them. And I know—I know—that's not enough.

"Combination," Nikolai calls.

I flow through a jump into a back camel spin, my arms extending in perfect form. It's strong, technically flawless. But I already know what's coming.

"Faster rotation," Nikolai says, then after a pause, "More expression."

I don't react, just nod, even though I already know it's useless. I need more expression, more artistry, more feeling.

I can land every jump, execute every spin with perfect placement. But the second I'm asked to sell it—to feel it—it all falls apart.

I glance at Nina and Zara. Nina's spins aren't as strong as mine, but she sells them. She makes them look effortless, like she's telling a story on the ice. Zara has a way of extending her arms just enough, of tilting her head at the perfect moment to make everything look intentional.

I know how to do the movements. But I don't know how to make people feel something when I do.

"Again," Nikolai calls.

I exhale, push into another spin. This time, I try—I try to extend my arms more gracefully, to make the movement look natural. But I can already feel it. It's forced. It doesn't feel like me.

I land my exit, and Nikolai watches me for a long moment before speaking.

"Technically perfect," he says. "But you are not an artist, Valeria. You are a machine. You need to be both."

It shouldn't sting. I already know this about myself. But somehow, it does.

I skate toward Nina, slowing my breathing. She bumps my shoulder. "He's just grumpy. You were incredible."

"Technically," I mutter.

Zara glides beside us. "I'll take your edges and jumps if you take my arms and face."

I let out a breath of laughter. "Deal."

"Cool down," Nikolai calls. "Then stretch."

I take a slow lap around the rink, feeling the exhaustion settle into my legs. Every drill today, I nailed. I was out in front, landing everything, showing exactly what I can do.

But none of it matters if I can't make people feel it.

I push harder into my final strokes, cutting into the ice. Maybe I don't need to. Maybe jumps and spins should be enough.

But Nikolai's voice lingers in my mind.

You are not an artist, Valeria. You are a machine. You need to be both.

Practice ends, and we are exhausted. Muscles burning, sweat cooling, breath still coming fast. We drop into stretches, letting the last of the tension seep from our bodies. The doors open, the familiar hum of the Zamboni kicking in as Harry moves onto the ice.

Normal. Expected. Routine.

Until—

"Hey, sis."

A man's voice. Deep. Familiar. Too familiar.

I freeze. That voice. I know that voice.

That's the voice that murmured against my skin, rough and hungry. The same voice that growled my name when his hands were gripping my waist, his body pressing into mine, his breath hot against my ear.

No. No. No.

"Hey, big brother," Nina responds.

No.

Nina's brother.

I stare straight ahead, my body rigid, my heartbeat hammering against my ribs, but I already know what's coming.

"Val! Come here! I want you to meet my brother!"

Before I can move, before I can think, Nina grabs my wrist and pulls me toward the open double doors. My body stumbles forward, my brain stuck.

I see him before he sees me.

Ethan.

The same Ethan whose hands had traced fire down my spine. The same Ethan whose mouth had left me breathless. The same Ethan I was supposed to never see again.

He turns just as Nina throws her arms around him, squeezing him tight in the way only a little sister can.

And then his eyes meet mine.

A flicker of something—recognition then realization. A pause, sharp and fleeting. A single breath held a second too long before his face smooths over. Meanwhile, my entire body feels like it's short-circuiting.

Nina beams between us, completely oblivious.

"Val! This is my big brother, Ethan! Ethan, this is Val. I can't believe you never got the chance to meet. I meant to introduce you two at the party!"

No one says a thing.

I can't move, can't even breathe.

My stomach drops and my pulse pounds so loud I can barely hear anything else. The cold air feels sharper now, the rink suddenly too small, too bright, too much.

Ethan doesn't react—not really. He stands there, hands in his pockets, shoulders loose and casual. Like this is just another introduction. Like this is just another day. Like this is just nothing.

But it's not nothing.

Because I feel it. The same pull I felt last night. The same low heat curling in my stomach, sharp and immediate. He's still devastatingly handsome—tall, broad, built like he's spent his entire life working with his hands. His dark hair is slightly tousled, his jaw sharp, his mouth a little too perfect. And his eyes—those deep, unreadable eyes that had locked on mine in the dark, just before he kissed me like he was starving.

That mouth was on mine. That body was pressed against me. I only knew his name. Nothing else.

Nina had talked about her older brother before, but I never paid attention, never asked for details. He's married. When he's not at work he'd spending time with his daughter.

Now I know exactly who he is. And he knows exactly what we did. *Wait, MARRIED?* My thoughts start to spiral, I'd slept with a married man.

I swallow hard. Nope. Not thinking about that.

I need to say something, anything. But my mouth refuses to work, my brain refuses to function, and all I can do is stand here, staring, as reality crashes down on me.

Ethan Crosse. Nina's older brother.

The man who had his hands on me. The man who had me gasping, unraveling, breaking beneath him.

I slept with Nina's older brother. Nina's *married* older brother.

This isn't happening. It can't be happening.

But it is.

And there's no way out.

Holy. Shit.

Four

Ethan

"NINA. WE NEED TO talk about adding a jump to your long program," her coach calls.

"Duty calls," Nina says, flashing a grin as she skates backward. "I'll see you two later."

I watch her go, the sound of her blades scraping clean against the ice. I was supposed to cut the rink, but Harry told me to wait.

"We need to talk," Valeria says.

She's tense, too tense, shoulders squared, jaw set, but her eyes give her away.

She's freaking out.

And I have a feeling I know why.

I watch as Valeria steps off the ice, sliding her blade guards over her skates with quick, sharp movements. Then, completely catching me off guard, she yanks me around the corner by my wrist.

"You're Nina's older brother?" Her voice is low, but sharp. Like she can't believe she's even saying the words. "How the hell did I not put two and two together?"

I don't know if I should answer. I don't know what she wants to hear. So I don't. I wait. My jaw tightens, my breath steady, but there's something uneasy curling in my chest. The silence stretches, heavy, and I hold it—watching, waiting.

She glances around, scanning the area like someone might overhear us, like we're standing on top of something that could explode at any second.

"Don't you have anything to say for yourself?" she snaps. "Why didn't you say anything?!"

I really don't like her tone. It feels like she's used to cutting people down with words, but I'm not some kid she can scold. I don't flinch. I don't move, if anything, my gaze hardens.

"Guess it never came up," I say, keeping my voice even.

She mutters something under her breath, shaking her head. "Unbelievable."

Then, something shifts. The anger doesn't disappear, but something else pushes through—panic.

"You're married," Valeria says, her voice lower now, but desperate. "We cannot tell Nina."

I don't even blink, although I'd be lying if I said it didn't sting, I was under the impression that we'd hit it off last night. "Wasn't planning on telling her anything."

She exhales sharply, still pacing, still running through whatever worst-case scenarios are playing in her head.

"I mean it, Ethan. We have to act like nothing happened," she says, spinning back to face me.

I raise a brow, watching her practically unravel in real time. "Well, you're not doing a great job being inconspicuous."

She glares. She liked me well enough to let me fuck her last night, but apparently she's embarrassed by that now? It doesn't make sense, but I'm not going to argue with her.

"We need to pretend that we're just..." she trails off, jaw tight.

I push off the wall slightly, leaning in just a little too close. "Just what?"

She exhales hard, like she has to force the word out. "Friends."

I let that settle. Just long enough to see how much she hates saying it. "Whatever you say," I reply, neutral.

She looks calmer now. Steadier, like she's convinced herself she's got this under control. Then, just as she turns to leave—

She stops. Freezes.

"You're married." She's repeating herself now.

Silence.

She looks at me. Waiting for me to correct her. Waiting for me to say something—anything—that will make this better.

I don't.

"Fuck!" The panic isn't just in her voice now—it's all over her face. Wide eyes. Uneven breathing. Hands curling into fists. She's spiraling.

"Okay, okay, calm down, Valeria," I say, keeping my voice low, steady.

She laughs, but it's sharp, humorless and frantic. "How am I supposed to calm down? I slept with someone's husband!"

I watch her carefully, my own chest feeling tighter now. She doesn't deserve this guilt.

"You weren't wearing a ring," she mutters, more to herself than to me. Then she looks up, right at me, her voice quieter but heavier. "I didn't think I needed to ask."

A pause. Then, softer—not just angry this time, but betrayed. "Why didn't you tell me you were married?"

I exhale, jaw clenching for a second before I meet her gaze. "Because I'm not. Okay, technically I am, but I'm not," I say, my voice tight.

Valeria folds her arms, jaw set. "What does that even mean?"

"It's a long story."

She doesn't miss a beat. "I have time. And you owe me the explanation."

I exhale sharply. Fine. She wants answers? She's getting them.

"Margo is my wife. She wanted to tour with her old band. She promised it would only be a couple of months and that she'd call, but she stopped calling. It's been a year. I haven't heard from her. My daughter hasn't heard from her. So I filed for divorce. She was served with the papers. Now I'm just waiting for her to sign them. It's been over for a long time. Yeah, I'm married, but I'm doing everything I can to end that."

Valeria doesn't move. She just stares, expression unreadable.

Then—her voice sharpens. "So what? Your wife leaves to go fulfill her dreams, and you just move on? Just like that?"

My jaw tightens. That's not how it was. "I didn't move on just like that, and she didn't leave just to fulfill her dreams. It's more complicated than that." I try to keep my voice steady, but I already know it's a losing battle.

Valeria's laugh is sharp, biting. "Could've fooled me. Seems like you moved on pretty easily."

The air shifts between us. Hotter. Heavier.

I feel my patience slipping, my pulse kicking up. "You don't know what you're talking about."

She tilts her head, eyes narrowing, but there's no cruelty in them—just sharpness, just doubt. "Then tell me I'm wrong."

I don't.

Instead, I step in closer, my voice lower now. "This is sounding less and less like someone who had a one-night stand and more like someone who wants something more."

Her eyes snap to mine, sharp as a blade. "You're delusional."

"Am I?" I challenge, watching her closely now, watching the way she tenses, the way her breath catches before she locks it down. "Because you sure as hell care a lot for someone who's trying so hard to stay detached."

Her jaw clenches, her breath unsteady. "I have no pity for cheaters. Nor would I ever have feelings for one."

That hits. So fucking hard I see red.

She doesn't get it. She doesn't get it at all. It's like she's already decided what's true, and nothing I say is going to change that.

I should stop. I should walk away. But something about her—about the way she's looking at me, like she's better than me, like I'm nothing—makes me want to hit back harder. I want her to hurt the way I do. I want her to feel it.

My voice is sharp, lethal. "You're what? 23 and up until last night, you were a virgin. I wonder if there's a reason for that?"

The second the words leave my mouth, I know I fucked up beyond repair.

She goes completely still.

For a second, I think she's just going to walk away. That she's going to be the bigger person. That I got the last word.

But then—

Her chest rises, slow and controlled, like she's deciding whether or not to say what she's about to say. Like she knows it'll ruin everything, and she's choosing to do it anyway.

Her lips part slightly, and something shifts in her eyes. Not just anger. Something colder. Sharper.

And then she destroys me.

"No wonder your wife left," she whispers.

It hits like a gunshot.

I stagger back a step, my lungs locking up, my body refusing to move, refusing to react, refusing to do anything but feel the weight of those five words.

Valeria doesn't wait for me to recover. She turns and walks out, her steps sharp, final.

I don't move. I don't breathe. I was already wounded, but this? This guts me.

A hand claps on my shoulder. Firm. Steady.

Harry. Joanne stands a few steps behind him, arms crossed, watching me carefully.

"She's tough, son," Harry says, voice gruff but knowing. "But I've never heard her that worked up. You got under her skin, but she didn't mean that. I know she's regretting it now."

I shake my head. "Doesn't matter. I shouldn't have said what I said back to her."

Harry exhales through his nose, nodding once. "Maybe not. But what's done is done."

Joanne adds, her voice softer, reassuring. "Give it time."

Harry watches me for a second, then gestures toward the door. "Why don't you take the rest of the morning off? We're not busy."

I hesitate. Then, I nod. And I leave.

I go straight to Drew's.

I work here five days a week. I love this job, I always have. I just wish it was enough so that I never had to take the second job. I wish I didn't need to keep stretching myself thin just to make things work.

But now? Now, I'm thinking of quitting the rink more than ever.

The garage is quiet this early, the overhead lights humming. The scent of motor oil and metal lingers in the air—familiar, grounding, steady. The kind of thing you can count on.

Rows of neatly organized tools line the walls, every wrench and socket exactly where it belongs. Simple. No guessing. No surprises. The Camaro Drew's been rebuilding sits in the center of the bay, hood up, parts scattered over the workbench like an unfinished puzzle.

I exhale slowly, letting the smell of grease and old leather settle over me. Trying to let it steady me.

This place has always been a second home. You fix what's broken. You tighten the bolts. You put in the work, and it pays off.

By the end of the day, there's something to show for it.

Unlike everything else in my life.

Drew barely glances up from under the hood of the Camaro as I walk in, wiping grease off his hands with an old rag.

"What's up, man?" he says, voice easy, distracted.

I don't answer right away. Just drop onto the couch, elbows on my knees, staring at the floor like it might have the answers I need.

"Nothing really," I mutter. "Just found out my one-night stand was Nina's best friend."

Drew freezes. The rag stills in his hands. Then, slowly, he straightens and looks at me. "Wait, what?" His brow furrows. "Start from the one-night stand part."

I blow out a breath, raking a hand through my hair. "Last night. Before I left the party, I ran into her—Valeria. She actually spilled her drink on me," I pause, the memory flickering back—the sharpness in her eyes, the way she looked at me like she already knew I was a mistake but was willing to make it anyway. "We talked. Didn't plan on leaving together, but it happened."

Drew leans against the workbench, arms crossed, watching me like I'm about to drop the real bomb.

"We hooked up," I continue, voice flat. "Thought it was a one-time thing. No details. Just...whatever it was."

"Alright..." Drew drawls, nodding along. "And?"

"And today, I walk into the rink and see her standing there—not just at the rink. On the ice. Skating like she owns the damn place. Turns out she's not just some girl I met at a party. She's Valeria Blaze. Figure skating prodigy. The one Harry's been raving about. The same Valeria Blaze who happens to be Nina's best friend."

Drew lets out a long, low whistle. "Shit."

"Yeah."

"And she didn't mention any of that last night?"

"Not a damn word." I shake my head, laughing dryly. "Neither did I, to be fair."

Drew smirks, but it fades just as fast. "So, what? You two just acted like it never happened?"

I tilt my head back, staring at the ceiling. "Not exactly. She panicked when she saw me. It was a whole thing. Then we argued, because apparently, I'm the asshole for existing in the same space as her now."

Drew lifts an eyebrow. "That bad?"

I let out a sharp exhale, shaking my head. "Worse. First, she realizes I'm still married, and she just—looks at me like I did something wrong. Like I'm some kind of liar." I lean forward, rubbing a hand over my jaw. "She says I should've told her last night, like I was supposed to sit her down in the middle of—" I cut myself off, shaking my head. "I don't know. Do a full background check before we hooked up?"

Drew smirks, but it's mild, more curiosity than amusement. "And what, she thinks you're just out here screwing around now?"

"Pretty much." I let out a bitter laugh. "She says I'm just 'moving on' like it's nothing. Like I'm the kind of guy who shrugs off a failed marriage and goes looking for a rebound." My fingers tighten against my knees.

Drew exhales, shaking his head. "She doesn't get it."

"No, she doesn't," I agree, voice tight. Then I huff out a breath, forcing myself to relax. "Not that I made it any better."

Drew gives me a look. "What'd you say?"

I rub the back of my neck, already bracing for the judgment. "I might've... made a comment."

"Ethan."

I sigh. "I said something about her being an ice queen. That maybe there's a reason she's never been in a real relationship."

Drew winces. "Damn. Alright, yeah, that's bad. But still—"

"Oh, it gets worse," I cut in. "Because then she fires back with, 'No wonder your wife left you.'"

Drew's head snaps toward me. His expression shifts—no smirk now, just understanding that this hit deep.

Silence stretches between us, thick and heavy.

I let out a humorless laugh, but there's no amusement in it. "Yeah. Hell of a first conversation, right?"

Drew exhales slowly, shaking his head. "Alright, so she went for the jugular."

I nod. "She didn't miss, either."

Drew leans back against the workbench, arms crossed, watching me. "And?"

"And what?"

"What are you gonna do about it?"

I stare at the ground for a beat, jaw tight. "Nothing. She made it clear what she thinks of me. Not much else to say."

Drew hums, but doesn't push. He just tosses the grease rag over his shoulder and goes back to the Camaro, like he's giving me space to sit with it.

And I do. But it doesn't feel any better.

Five
Valeria

INSTEAD OF THINKING ABOUT that night, I bury myself in training.

I lose count of the days that pass. I just do whatever it takes to avoid Ethan Crosse.

He infuriates me. Not just because of what he said, not just because it hurt. But because I know I went too far. I know I shouldn't have dragged his marriage into it.

I feel awful about that. I know I need to apologize, but I'm not ready to face him.

So, I do what I always do. I push myself until there's nothing left to feel. Until exhaustion drowns out everything else. I wrap my ankles, tape them, and lace my skates so tight my feet tingle. Whatever it takes to stay upright. Whatever it takes to stay in control.

"Okay, girly! Lunch time," Nina sing-songs, stepping into the room with her little lunch box, looking far too cheerful for how drained I feel.

Part of training at the rink means being involved—helping out in the box office, doing chores around the rink, really whatever they need. So, on Saturdays I practically live here. It's really not that bad.

Thankfully, I don't have to do anything with the skating school, that's all Nina. I can only imagine the chaos that's waiting for her out there.

"You gonna eat?" Nina asks, already unzipping her lunch bag.

"Yeah," I say automatically. "I'm just gonna wash my hands and face. You go ahead. You have to be on the ice soon."

She nods, already digging into her food, and I slip away to the bathroom.

The cold water feels sharp against my skin as I splash it over my face. When I straighten, I catch my reflection in the mirror.

My landings today were sloppy. Too much impact. Too much drag. I'm skating seven days a week now that Nationals are closing in.

I have to stay focused. I have to be lighter. Faster. More efficient.

Lunch isn't going to help with that.

So I skip it.

I'm sorting through papers in the box office when Nina bursts in, out of breath.

"Joanne, there are two beginner classes, but I'm the only coach assigned," she says frantically.

Joanne looks up from her desk, frowning. "Oh shoot. I forgot the city added a class. How many kids?"

"Sixteen." Nina exhales hard. "Too many for me to give them individual attention. And the parents are already getting impatient."

Joanne sighs, rubbing her temples. "Okay, let me try to call another coach in. I can see if anyone's available—"

"I can do it," I say, cutting her off.

Joanne blinks. "Really?"

"Yeah," I shrug. "You're in a lurch. I can do it."

A beat of silence. Then— "Thank you so much, Valeria," Joanne says, relief flooding her voice.

Nina exhales like the weight of the world has been lifted off her shoulders. "Seriously, Val, you're a lifesaver."

I nod, already moving. Helping. Staying busy. Doing what I always do.

Because it's easier than stopping.

Easier than thinking.

Easier than feeling.

Easier than facing the fact that Nationals are creeping closer, and for the first time in my life, I don't know if I'm good enough.

I never took my skates off, so I head straight to the ice, sliding off my guards before stepping on. The familiar bite of the blade against the surface sends a small shiver up my spine, but I push it away.

Nina looks overwhelmed. I can see it in the way she waves her arms, trying to corral the group. The kids aren't listening, they're skating everywhere, weaving in and out, giggling, and bumping into each other. One almost topples over, and Nina lunges to grab them just in time.

I skate up to her, and as soon as I do, a hush settles over the class.

It's not me. It's my presence. My demeanor. I have that effect on people, I always have. I don't have to raise my voice. I don't have to tell them to pay attention.

They just do.

"Thanks, Val," Nina says, a little breathless.

"No problem. Let's just get class going." I fold my arms, scanning the group as Nina starts running through the warm-up drills.

I'm here, but I'm not.

My body feels light, disconnected, like I'm floating somewhere between exhaustion and habit. The rink sounds blur—Nina's voice, the scrape of skates, the occasional burst of laughter from the younger kids. My fingers twitch at my sides, a phantom ache settling in my limbs, but I ignore it.

Then I see her.

A little girl.

She's small, practically buzzing with energy, moving with a kind of quiet determination that sets her apart. Her blonde ponytail bounces with every stride, stray waves slipping free and catching the rink lights. Her dress is bright, covered in glitter and color, bold in a way that makes her impossible to ignore.

But it's not her appearance that holds my attention.

It's the way she skates.

While the others follow the drills in loose, wobbly strides, she's doing something else. Each time she falters she adjusts, focuses, and pushes herself.

Her edges cut into the ice, some turns too deep, others too shallow. She isn't afraid of speed, isn't afraid to push past what's comfortable, but there's no hesitation in her movements. She lifts into a one-foot glide, holding it longer than she should be able to before shifting into a shaky crossover. It's too advanced for this class, too much for what Nina's teaching.

But she doesn't stop.

She isn't showing off. She isn't playing.

She's skating like it's the only thing that matters.

She miscalculates slightly. Her balance wavers, her edges slip, but she recovers before she falls. Her brows furrow, lips pressing together, frustration flickering across her face.

She hates failing.

I know that feeling. Because I was the same way.

I glance at the other kids, their laughter filling the rink, their movements easy and unbothered. They skate because it's fun. Because it's new. Because they have nothing to prove.

I should be helping the others. I should be making sure Nina isn't overwhelmed, but my focus narrows. I don't mean to ignore the rest of the class, don't mean to leave Nina handling a dozen kids on her own, but luckily, some of the older skaters step in, guiding the others through the basics.

It gives me a moment. Just one.

And I take it.

I push off, gliding toward her, watching the way she leans forward, arms stiff, every muscle in her body focused on getting it right. She doesn't notice me at first, too locked into the challenge in front of her.

I match her pace, skating beside her, waiting for her to react.

Her green eyes flick toward me for a second before snapping back ahead. Determined. Focused. But I catch the flicker of excitement, the way she straightens slightly, like the presence of someone else makes this more than just practice.

It makes it a challenge.

She speeds up.

So I do too.

Her breath quickens as she digs into her crossovers, edges cutting harder, movements sharper. I let her take the lead, let her feel it for a few seconds—until I push off harder, overtaking her in smooth, effortless strokes.

She exhales sharply, frustration flashing across her face.

I smirk. "You almost had me."

She huffs, cheeks flushed, but she's grinning. "I wasn't done yet."

I slow, extending a hand. "Then let's do it again."

She takes in a firm, confident grip.

"Alright," I say, "but this time, keep your knees softer when you push off."

She nods quickly, already eager, already in motion. She's light on her feet, but her technique is raw—too much power in the wrong places, not enough control in others. She gets ahead of herself, chasing speed instead of precision.

I let her go for a few strides, watching the way her pony-tail bounces with each push, the way she throws herself into her crossovers too soon, edges slicing deeper than they should.

She stumbles, a misstep that throws her balance for half a second.

I catch up instantly, my stride steady, my presence beside her enough to make her refocus. "Relax," I say, voice even, just loud enough for her to hear over the scrape of skates.

She exhales, but this time, her shoulders drop slightly, her arms loosen.

"Again," I say. "Don't force it. Feel it."

She doesn't argue, just pushes forward. This time, her movements smooth out, the rough edges of her technique sharpening, refining, as she matches my rhythm.

The others are still doing their drills in the background, but here, it feels like just the two of us.

She watches me carefully, mirroring my weight shifts, pushing off—not just with speed, but with control.

She isn't just skating; she's studying every movement, every shift of weight, every mistake and correction. She watches the ice the way I used to, not just for where she's going but for what she can learn. She wants to be better, to push herself.

The realization settles deep in my chest, something un-spoken rising to the surface, something I haven't felt in years. I remember chasing after my coaches on the ice, desperate to prove I could keep up, that I belonged.

And now, she's chasing after me.

I slow, testing her reaction. She slows too, unconsciously mirroring me, her instincts already adjusting.

I meet her eyes. "Better."

Her entire face lights up, green eyes shining like I just handed her a trophy. "Again?" she asks, breathless.

I nod. "Again."

And we keep skating.

Time flies by, the minutes blurring together as the class moves through their drills. I don't pay attention to the clock, but I can feel it in the way the kids are slowing down, their initial energy fading into tired but satisfied movements. Nina's voice rises and falls over the sound of blades scraping against the ice, her instructions mixing with laughter and the occasional stumble.

The little girl is still skating, still pushing herself harder than the others, still chasing something only she can see.

Before I can think about it too much, Nina claps her hands, her voice cutting through the last few moments of practice.

"Okay, kids! Class is over," Nina calls, clapping her hands.

She skates over, still slightly out of breath from trying to keep up with everyone.

"Hey! Val, I see you met my niece, Cassidy," she says, grinning.

I blink, my chest tightening. "Cassidy? As in Cassidy Crosse?"

"Yeah," Nina says. "CC has wanted to learn how to skate forever! Ethan finally gave in and let her take classes."

Ethan's daughter.

My stomach drops.

I look down at CC, who's still beaming, completely unaware of the way my world just tilted.

"Nice to meet you, CC," My throat feels tight. "I gotta go."

Her face falls just slightly, but she nods, accepting it without protest.

I hesitate, something twisting in my chest. I don't know what to say, don't know how to make this moment mean what it feels like it should. But I can give her this—one thing I wish someone had told me when I was her age.

"You did great out there," I say, my voice quieter, but steady. "Keep skating."

Her eyes brighten, her small hands gripping the barrier beside her. "Really?"

I nod. "Yeah. You've got something special. Don't stop. But uh... I gotta go."

I don't wait for her to respond. I don't wait for Nina to question it.

My heart is pounding, my breath too shallow, my body suddenly too aware of itself in a way I can't explain.

Ethan's daughter? No way. I can't do this.

I step off the rink, peeling off my gloves with a little too much force, but that's when I see him.

Ethan. Standing there. Watching me.

His expression is unreadable at first, but when I meet his gaze, I recognize it immediately.

He looks pissed.

And he has every right to be.

I consider walking past him, pretending I don't see him, but I know that won't work. It's better to just face it, to bite the bullet before it gets worse.

I make my way toward him, feeling every second of the distance between us.

"Ethan," I start, forcing myself to meet his eyes. "I've been thinking about what I said a lot. I'm so sorry. That was below the belt. I was hurt, and I didn't mean it."

For a moment, he says nothing.

His jaw tenses, his lips press into a thin line. Then, finally—

"I'm sorry too," he says. "I shouldn't have said what I said either. I was mad."

That's it. No drawn-out lecture. No need to make me grovel. Just an acknowledgment, an understanding that we both went too far.

Before either of us can say anything else, Nina barrels into the moment, full force as usual.

"Good, I caught you!" She grins like she's been waiting for this exact opportunity. "We're having a family dinner at my parents' house tonight. I know I've asked you before, and you always say no. Please! I really want you to come, and CC agrees."

I hesitate, glancing at Ethan.

I've never gone before. I've always had an excuse. Too busy, too tired, too focused on skating. But maybe I should go this time.

"Okay. I'll come," I say, surprising even myself.

Nina squeals, literally squeals, and happy-dances her way to the locker room before I can change my mind.

I turn back to Ethan.

It feels like a fresh start. Like maybe this can be different.

"We'll talk later," I say, offering him the out.

"No need," he replies, a flicker of something in his eyes I can't quite place. "All is forgiven, Valeria. See you tonight."

Then he looks down at CC, who has been watching this entire exchange with careful curiosity.

"Come on, squirt. Let's head out," he says, ruffling her blonde hair.

"Thank you, Ms. Blaze! I'll see you next week!" CC chirps, grinning up at me.

I nod, forcing a smile, but my chest still feels tight.

Ethan and CC walk off together, her small hand swinging in his as she chatters excitedly, practically bouncing with every step. He listens, nodding along, throwing in a teasing remark every so often that makes her giggle.

I should leave. I should be walking in the opposite direction, shaking off whatever this is before it settles.

But I don't.

I watch.

The way he slows his steps to match hers, the way he adjusts her ponytail absentmindedly when it starts slipping loose, the way he makes her feel like the most important person in the world without even trying.

It's effortless for him. Not forced or performed, just... who he is.

And I feel something shift, something I don't like.

I knew Ethan was a father. I knew he loved his daughter. But seeing it is different. Feeling it is different. Watching him hold her hand like it's the most unshakable thing in his life, like there's nowhere else he'd rather be, like he'd rearrange the entire universe to make sure she felt safe—

It's disarming.

Because it tells me everything about the kind of person he is.

And I like him.

Not just in the abstract, not just in the physical way I spent an entire night trying to forget. I like him in a way I wasn't expecting, in a way I didn't see coming, in a way I don't know how to stop.

And that should be my cue to walk away.

To bury it. To shut it down before it turns into something I can't control.

But I don't.

And maybe that's the real problem.

Six
Ethan

As CC AND I leave the rink, she's chatting up a storm, but I can't listen. My mind is somewhere else. On Valeria.

The way she worked with CC, the way she pushed her but still showed kindness. I saw a side of her I hadn't expected—steady, patient, strong.

She gave that side of herself to CC. With me, it's different. Guarded. Like she's holding something back.

I shouldn't be thinking about her like this. I can't. She's Nina's best friend. I'm a single father. She has her whole life ahead of her, and I'm still untangling myself from a marriage that failed.

A failure.

"Are we going to Grandma and Grandpa's for dinner?" CC asks, practically bouncing in her seat.

"Yeah, squirt. We're going tonight," I reply.

We pull into our driveway, and before I even put the truck in park, CC is already unbuckling herself, hopping out before I can tell her to slow down.

I follow her up the porch, boots creaking against the old wood. The front yard looks the same as ever—patchy grass, garden gnomes CC and Nina thought were funny, a porch that could use another coat of paint. I keep telling myself that I'll fix it. Mom says I need to. Dad says it's fine the way it is.

The screen door slams shut behind me with its usual clang. Inside, the air smells like leftover takeout and stale coffee, maybe a hint of the cinnamon candle CC made me buy last week.

The living room is the usual mess. CC's toys are scattered across the floor, books stacked half-open where she left them. One of them, a fairy tale book Nina gave her, rests on the couch with a crumpled blanket beside it, left where CC and I curled up reading last night. The couch cushions are lopsided from our last movie night, and there's a smudge of peanut butter on the coffee table. I swipe at it with my thumb, shaking my head.

"CC, don't eat too much," I warn as she heads straight for the kitchen, already rummaging through the fridge.

I bend down to grab her bag and toss it on the hook in the mudroom.

By the time I step into the kitchen, CC is peeling an orange at the table, feet swinging beneath her chair.

"Did you see how fast I was going today?" she asks, already mid-story, her face lighting up as she talks.

I grab a bottle of water from the fridge and lean against the counter, listening.

I don't understand half the moves she talks about, the jumps, the spins, the way she breaks it all down like a puzzle she's constantly solving. But I know that look in her eyes. The way her whole face lights up, like nothing else in the world matters.

That's enough for me.

"Okay, hop in the shower! We're heading to Grandma's!" I cheer.

I'm sure Nina is already there, helping Mom cook.

I sit on the couch, scrolling through my phone, but I don't have to wait long. CC comes bounding down the stairs, dressed and ready, a brush in her hands. I already know what's coming.

She stops in front of me, holding it up like an offering. "Can you do my hair, Daddy?"

"Of course, sweetheart," I say, taking the brush from her. "What do you want?"

"Braids, please!" she exclaims.

"You got it," I say, patting the spot in front of me so she can sit.

I start to braid her hair, fingers working through the familiar motions. I love doing this. *Always have.* But lately, it feels different. She's growing up too fast, her hair longer, her patience shorter.

She used to sit still for this, small and content in my lap, insisting I make her look like a princess. Now, she barely sits still at all, already halfway out the door before I can remind her to grab a jacket.

I twist another section of hair, securing it carefully, and something in my chest tightens.

She tilts her head slightly, checking her reflection in the nearby mirror. "Looks good," she says with a satisfied nod.

Margo should be here for this. The thought hits me like a truck. She should be the one sitting behind CC, combing through the knots, braiding her hair, telling her how beautiful she looks. *But she isn't. And she never will be, not in the way CC needs.*

CC deserves a mother. *A real one. Someone who shows up, someone who stays, someone who puts her first. But Margo doesn't deserve a daughter like CC.*

And the worst part is, *CC knows it too.* She never asks about her anymore. Never wonders when she's coming home. Never looks for her in the stands.

She just keeps moving forward.

I tie off the braid and smooth my hand over the top of her head.

She leans into my touch for half a second before springing up, already onto the next thing, already racing toward the door.

I push myself up, shaking off the weight in my chest. "Alright, squirt. Let's hit the road."

Family dinners have been a thing for as long as I can remember. Every Saturday night, no exceptions.

And somehow, it's still the same excitement from CC.

She's bouncing in her seat as I pull up to my parents' driveway. The smell of woodsmoke and roasting chicken drifts through the cool evening air, curling from the open windows, a welcome aroma that promises a warm evening.

The house comes into view, a large farmhouse standing against the backdrop of open land and towering trees. The soft cream exterior, accented by navy blue shutters, looks exactly as it always has—sturdy, familiar, the kind of place that never changes no matter how much life does. The paint is beginning to wear in some places, but that only adds to its character.

The wraparound porch stretches wide, its weathered wooden railings lined with potted flowers that Mom fusses over, her way of making sure the house feels as welcoming as ever. Rocking chairs sit in their usual spots, ready for conversation, for slow evenings spent watching the land roll out around us.

Beyond the house, the yard extends into a well-tended vegetable garden and the small chicken coop my dad still insists is more useful than it probably is. A gravel driveway leads past the house to the detached garage and workshop, where he spends half his time tinkering, fixing things that don't need fixing, just for the sake of keeping his hands busy.

My dad, bless his old heart, parks in the usual spot, close enough to the porch that she doesn't have to struggle with the car door. Mom always complains, but I bet she secretly appreciates the convenience.

Besides Ryan and Drew's vehicles, there aren't any other cars. Ryan Porter and Drew Miller have been my best friends since childhood. They're family at this point and at every family dinner laughing, arguing, and enjoying every bit of it.

We step out of the truck and CC races for the porch.

"Grandpa! Grandma!" she calls, already halfway across the yard.

I watch her, a soft smile tugging at my lips.

"Slow down, squirt," I shout after her.

Her laughter echoes off the trees nearby.

I stop at the top step, breathing in the cool evening air, feeling the warmth radiating from CC's vibrant energy. She's all sunshine in this moment.

Maybe, just maybe, tonight could be a night like the good ones.

I follow CC inside and look around for everyone. She darts past me, already making her way toward the kitchen, her sights set on whatever snack she can sneak before dinner. I take my time, letting the familiarity settle over me.

This house never changes. And I wouldn't want it to.

"Grandma! Grandpa!" CC yells again.

"Lovebug!" Dad exclaims. He picks up CC and twirls her around, her laughter filling the space like it belongs there. Like it always has.

Dad sets her back down, ruffling her hair before turning to me, that knowing look in his eyes. The same look he always had when I was a kid, standing in his garage, waiting for him to teach me something new.

Grant Crosse is the man who taught me everything I know. I grew up watching him work, handing him wrenches before I even knew what they were for, listening as he explained how machines fit together, how patience and precision could fix almost anything. *He gave me a piece of himself in every lesson, every scraped knuckle, every late night spent side by side in the garage.*

I love him for that.

And no matter how much time passes, no matter how much life changes, I know one thing will always be true—he's the kind of man I can count on.

"Hi, sweetie. Did you enjoy skating?" Mom asks, her voice warm as she brushes a hand over CC's hair.

Hannah Crosse. My mother has made this house a home. She raised us, kept us steady, made sure we never went without. Every dinner was homemade, every scraped knee tended to, every late-night homework session met with patience and encouragement.

But she didn't just pour herself into us—she poured herself into everyone. She's always been that way, the kind of woman who remembers birthdays, who organizes fundraisers for neighbors in need, who somehow has time to volunteer at the school and still make it home in time to put a full meal on the table.

I watch as she fusses over CC, the same way she used to fuss over me and Nina.

CC, still bouncing with energy, looks up at Dad. "Grandpa, did you hear about my spin today?"

Dad chuckles, resting a hand on her shoulder. "Your dad told me you nailed it. That true?"

CC nods fiercely. "Uh-huh! Ms. Valeria saw too! She said it was solid!"

At that, my eyes flick to the woman in question, who's been standing quietly nearby. She shifts slightly, like she's not used to being pulled into the family's rhythm. But there's something in her expression—something softer.

"That right?" Dad asks, glancing at Valeria with that steady, assessing look he gives everyone. The kind that reads people before they even realize they're being read.

Valeria meets his gaze without hesitation. "She's got a natural feel for the ice," she says simply. "If she keeps working, she'll only get better."

CC beams. "Hear that, Grandpa? I'm gonna be just like Val!"

Dad grins, nudging her lightly. "You work half as hard as she does, and you just might."

Valeria doesn't react right away, but I see the flicker of something in her eyes.

"Valeria's the best skater ever," CC announces proudly, turning to Mom. "Right, Grandma?"

Mom laughs, ever the peacemaker. "I think she's pretty incredible."

Valeria lets out a small breath, then clears her throat. "Thanks," she says, a little hesitant, like she's not sure what to do with the praise.

"Let's eat, everyone!" Mom says.

We all head to the dining room. The table is packed, everything laid out like always—roast chicken, buttery mashed potatoes, green beans tossed with garlic, fresh dinner rolls that are still warm from the oven. Mom made her famous mac and cheese, the kind with the crispy top that CC always fights for.

I take a seat and look around. Drew. Nina. Ryan. Valeria. Everyone is here.

My eyes keep drifting to Valeria, she's beautiful. That's not news. But standing here, in my parents' home, in something softer, something warmer than her skating clothes, I catch myself looking too long.

We all dig in and begin to eat. The table is loud, everyone talking over each other like they always do, the kind of noise that used to drive me crazy as a teenager but now feels like home.

Ryan is the first to speak, mouth half-full like always. "Alright, let's settle this now. Greatest movie trilogy of all time. And if anyone says anything other than the original *Star Wars*, they can leave."

Drew scoffs, reaching for another roll. "That's predictable. *Lord of the Rings* exists, you know."

"You mean the movies that take an hour just to get out of the damn Shire?" Ryan fires back.

"You have no taste," Nina chimes in, stabbing a piece of chicken. "*The Dark Knight* trilogy is superior."

Dad shakes his head, unimpressed, as he spoons mashed potatoes onto his plate. "Kids these days don't know what a real movie is. *Butch Cassidy and the Sundance Kid*. That's cinema."

I smirk, glancing at Valeria, who has barely said a word, just quietly observing the chaos. She's eating, but slower, taking small bites, like she's still deciding how she feels about the atmosphere. Or maybe the company.

"What do you think, Val?" I ask.

She looks up, eyes flicking between them all like she's analyzing a competition. "Objectively? *Lord of the Rings*. But I'd rather not start a war at the dinner table."

Ryan groans dramatically, tossing his fork onto his plate. "Et tu, Valeria?"

Nina grins, passing her the basket of rolls. "You'll fit in just fine."

She hesitates for a beat before taking one, fingers brushing lightly against mine as I reach for the same basket. She doesn't pull away immediately, and neither do I.

"You always this diplomatic?" I ask, voice low enough that only she hears.

She lifts a brow, the ghost of a smirk playing at the corner of her lips. "When necessary. But I can argue with the best of them."

"I don't doubt that," I murmur, watching the way she studies me, like she's still figuring me out.

She shifts slightly, pushing her plate forward, finished eating but still lingering. "Do you always ask deep, thought-provoking questions over dinner?"

I huff a quiet laugh. "Nah. Sometimes we discuss life's biggest mysteries, like why *Die Hard* is obviously a Christmas movie or how Ryan ever passed the bar exam."

"Because I'm brilliant," Ryan calls out, clearly eavesdropping.

"Debatable," Drew mutters, dodging a playful jab from Ryan.

Val shakes her head, amused, but there's something softer in her expression now. She's relaxed—just a little. I don't know what I expected when she agreed to come tonight, but seeing her here, actually engaging, is... nice.

She catches me watching her and tilts her head. "What?"

"Nothing," I say, shaking my head. "Just glad you're here."

Her gaze flickers before she looks away. She doesn't seem uncomfortable. Just thoughtful.

The conversation shifts again, the table still alive with debate and laughter. But for the first time tonight, I feel like Valeria isn't just an observer.

Dinner winds down, plates empty except for a few stray bites of mashed potatoes and the last roll CC is still eyeing. I lean back, full, content, until my gaze drifts across the table.

Valeria's plate barely looks touched.

The others had second helpings, clearing their plates without thinking twice. Hers? A few scraps of lettuce, a couple of berries, nothing else. No dressing, no toppings, nothing that makes a meal feel like a meal.

I frown, watching as she pushes the last piece of fruit around with her fork before setting it down like she's finished.

Like that was enough.

I don't say anything yet. But my appetite isn't as strong anymore.

"Boys, go in the living room while we clean," Mom says.

"Not happening, Mom," I say. "You cooked. We clean. Go relax."

We start clearing the table, passing plates, stacking dishes, the usual post-dinner routine we've done a hundred times before. Someone washes, someone dries, someone half-jokingly complains about the mess. It's quick, efficient, and second nature when you grew up around here.

By the time the last dish is set on the drying rack, Ryan stretches like he just did all the work, then heads to the fridge. "Alright, boys, who needs one?" He starts tossing out beers before anyone even answers.

I catch mine without thinking, the cold can familiar in my grip as we make our way to the den.

We settle in, the familiar routine easing in like it always does. The room smells like old leather and faint cigar smoke, the kind of place where conversations always go deeper than they should.

Dad leans back in his chair, eyes on me. "So, son, how's everything going with the divorce?"

I exhale, rubbing the back of my neck. "I don't really know." I glance at Ryan. "Have you heard anything?"

Ryan shakes his head, setting his beer down. "No. I know we served her, but nothing else. She hasn't signed or returned it with any stipulations."

My grip tightens on the can, jaw clenching. "I just want it done."

There's a heavy pause. We've all lived with the weight of Margo in some way. She's not here, but she still lingers in every decision.

Drew is the one to break the silence. "You think she's stalling on purpose?"

I shake my head, but the truth is, I don't know. "Wouldn't put it past her. But honestly? I don't know what she wants anymore. She had the chance to be a real wife, a real mother. She didn't take it."

Ryan folds his arms, leaning back. "She never really seemed like she wanted the family life. Did you know that before you married her?"

I stare at the label on my beer, peeling at the edge with my thumb. I don't answer right away.

Then, finally, I sigh. "Maybe. Maybe I didn't want to see it."

Dad nods, doesn't press. He lets the words settle.

But Drew and Ryan? They aren't done yet.

Ryan smirks, shifting the mood. "Well, at least you got good taste now. Valeria's way out of Margo's league."

I don't react. Or at least, I try not to.

Then Ryan leans forward, stretching out his legs like he's getting comfortable. "I was thinking about asking her out."

I freeze.

It's quick, instinctual almost, but it happens. My fingers flex just a little, and when I go to take a sip, I almost miss my mouth. Setting the bottle down harder than I mean to, my gaze shoots to my friend.

Drew notices first. "Huh."

I glance at him. "What?"

He shrugs, but the grin is already forming. "Nothing. Just... you made a face."

Dad chuckles, shaking his head. "He did."

Ryan raises an eyebrow, amused now. "Oh, you definitely did. Interesting."

I scoff. "I didn't make a damn face."

Drew leans forward, eyes locked on me like he's got me figured out. "So, what's going on with you and Valeria?"

"Nothing," I say too quickly.

Silence. No one buys it.

Dad takes a slow sip of his beer, then sets it down. "Then why does she make you look like you don't know what the hell to do with yourself?"

I rub a hand over my jaw, exhaling hard. I don't want to talk about this. Not here. Not now. But it's my dad and my brothers. There's no getting out of it.

I sigh. "I don't know, man."

That lands. No one speaks for a moment.

Then, Dad, ever steady, ever sure, watches me carefully. "What don't you know?"

I shake my head, frustrated. "She's different, the only girlfriend I've ever really had was Margo. I don't know what to do with that."

Drew smirks, like he's been waiting for this moment. "So it's not just a 'Nina's best friend' thing."

I grit my teeth. "It should be."

Dad doesn't say anything right away. He just watches me, like he's weighing his words. Then, finally, he speaks. "Maybe you're just not ready to admit it yet."

I take another drink, ignoring the way the words sit heavy in my chest.

Maybe he's right. And that's exactly the problem.

Because if he is, I'm screwed.

Seven
Valeria

IT'S OFFICIAL. FIFTEEN DAYS. No breaks. No real rest. Just ice, training, workouts, stretching, more training. My body feels it, but that's the point. That's the plan.

I step out of the shower, wrapping a towel around myself, steam curling against my skin. The mirror is fogged, but not enough to hide what's underneath. When I wipe my hand across the mirror and take myself in, I'm not sure how to feel.

I was always lean. Now, I'm just light. Too light. Or maybe just light enough. My arms don't look as strong as they used to, but they're not meant to be strong. They're meant to be elegant, refined, graceful. My collarbones cut sharper. My ribs press faintly against my skin when I exhale, each breath shallow and calculated.

I run my fingers along my hip bone, tracing the sharp edge of it. My stomach is flat and hollow, every last trace of softness gone. My legs, once quietly strong, feel different. Not weak. Just... less. Less to carry. Less to hold me down.

Still, it's not enough.

My jumps still feel heavy. My landings still sink too much into the ice. The rotations aren't where they should be. Every ounce matters. Every fraction of weight is a fraction of a second lost in the air.

I roll my shoulders, watching the way my body moves, how my skin pulls tight over muscle, how there's nothing extra left. It's closer. It's better. But it's not there yet.

Not yet.

I grip the edge of the sink, exhaling slowly. My body has always been built for precision. But precision isn't enough.

Precision needs freedom.

And freedom means lighter.

I can hear my parents downstairs. Mom is probably either cooking something or bringing in the chef to handle it. She loves to cook when she has time, but most of the time, she doesn't. If she's on a deadline, she barely steps foot in the kitchen.

She's a photographer. And not just any photographer—she's sought after, booked months in advance, her work printed in magazines, hanging in galleries, displayed in homes most people will never step foot in. She captures the world through her lens, but sometimes, I wonder if she even sees the one right in front of her.

Dad's the same way. An architect, in demand, always moving, always working. His buildings are known for their clean lines and detailed fixtures.

I grew up in a house designed by two people who see the world in frames and blueprints. Clean edges, perfect compositions, control in every decision.

And I was raised to fit into it. That's not to say they don't love me, they do. It's just that we're a different sort of family than Nina and hers.

I tighten the towel around me, shaking off the thought.

Downstairs, I hear my mom's laugh, light and effortless, my dad's voice steady beside her. They're home, but they're always somewhere else too.

That's just how it is.

I throw on something comfy—my go-to yoga pants and a sweatshirt. Even though my parents are formal, dinners at home are always casual. They love being able to just let loose. Well, to the best of their ability, that is.

Ana Lucia Blaze, my mom, is poised, always. Dark brown hair, streaked with gray, swept back in effortless waves. Her deep brown eyes hold warmth, but there's always something else beneath it—concern, calculation, quiet expectation. She moves with grace, every step measured, every glance thoughtful.

Emilio Blaze, my dad, is the same way. Tall, lean, his posture straight like it was trained into him. His dark hair, now threaded with gray, is neatly styled, adding to his polished demeanor. Even now, dressed in something casual for him—perfectly tailored slacks, a crisp shirt—he still looks ready for a business meeting. His warm brown eyes scan the room with quiet observation, never missing anything.

I step into the kitchen and pause.

The chef is already at work, plating what looks like an entire feast. Rich sauces, delicate garnishes, portions too precise to be homemade.

Fuck.

How am I supposed to just eat less?

"Hi, dear," my mom says, sweeping into the room, effortlessly put together like always. She gestures toward the chef. "This is Chef Laurent. He's preparing dinner tonight—last-minute booking, but I got lucky. He just finished a shoot with *Gastronome Weekly*."

The chef looks up briefly, nodding in greeting before returning to his work

"Hi, Mom," I reply, tearing my eyes away from the food, already calculating.

It all looks rich. Heavy. Too much.

We all settle around the dining table, the usual hum of conversation filling the space. The food is plated beautifully, steam rising, the scent of roasted garlic and warm bread thick in the air.

Before anyone reaches for their plates, the chef steps forward, hands folded neatly in front of him, his tone professional but easy.

"For tonight's dinner," he begins, "we have fresh baguette with whipped herb butter and sea salt, followed by a seasonal greens salad with lemon vinaigrette and toasted almonds. The main course is a roast chicken with garlic and thyme jus, served with parmesan mashed potatoes and sautéed green beans with shallots. And for dessert, an apple tart with vanilla bean ice cream."

A murmur of approval spreads around the table as plates are set down, warm rolls passed around, glasses filled. The meal is rich but familiar, something comforting without being extravagant.

Then the chef turns to me.

"And for you, Miss Blaze," he continues, his voice smooth, practiced. "Grilled chicken breast, lightly seasoned, with a side of steamed greens and roasted sweet potatoes. No butter, no oil, as requested. Your salad is without almonds, and the dressing is on the side. And for dessert, we have fresh fruit or yogurt, whichever you prefer."

Mom smiles, lifting her glass. "Honey, Chef prepared a separate meal for you. I know that you're eating a specialty diet."

"Thank you, Mom," I reply with a small smile. She always tries. I just don't know how to let her in.

I turn to the chef, polite, controlled. "Thank you," I say.

He nods and walks back to the kitchen to clean up.

It looks great. Smells even better.

I know I can eat the salad. So I eat that. I move on to the greens, finishing all of them. A few bites of chicken and potatoes. No more than that. Just enough.

And I feel it—satisfied. Full, even.

Which is exactly when my mother notices.

"Sweetheart, is that all you're having?" Her voice is light, but there's a hint of concern.

My father glances at my plate. "You should eat a little more, Valeria. You're training hard. You need the fuel."

I take another sip of water, slow and measured, even as my stomach feels too full, even as my pulse stays steady by force alone. "I am eating."

Mom gives me a small, approving smile, but I can see the hesitation in her eyes. Dad nods, satisfied enough, but I know them. I know how they work.

They notice everything.

The clink of silverware fills the silence. No chaotic sibling debates. No laughter. Just quiet, refined conversation. Controlled. Predictable.

Mom dabs at the corner of her mouth with her napkin. "How's training?"

"Good. Nikolai is pushing me harder than ever," I say, cutting my next bite of chicken smaller than necessary. "But that's nothing new."

Dad nods approvingly. "Discipline. That's what keeps you ahead."

Mom watches me for a moment longer, her expression unreadable. "Are you still keeping up with yoga?"

"Every morning," I reply.

She nods, satisfied. "Good. Balance is just as important as strength."

Dad cuts another piece of his chicken, his movements precise, efficient. "You'll be ready for Nationals." It's not a question. It's certainty.

I nod, setting my fork down. "I will be."

That's the end of it. They don't ask about anything else. They've always waiting for me to tell them more, it's something I appreciate about them.

It's not about how I feel. Not about exhaustion. Not about the toll of fifteen straight days on the ice. It's about results. About expectations. And nothing else matters.

They move on. Another bite. Another sip of wine. As if nothing is wrong.

And maybe nothing is.

Eight
Ethan

I ARRIVE AT THE rink, coffee in hand. Today was supposed to be my day off.

Joanne called me in because Harry is down with a cold and they needed someone to cover. I don't mind. It's not like I haven't done this a hundred times before, but I won't have to do it much longer.

The garage is picking up. Drew needs another person managing, and he's given me that position. It's good money. Stable. Something I can build on. I won't need the rink job to make ends meet anymore.

Still, this place has been good to me. It gave me work when I needed it, made sure my family was taken care of, helped Nina when we couldn't. Leaving is not as simple as just handing in my notice.

But it is time.

I push open the office door, stepping inside to find Joanne at her desk.

"Hey. Do you have a minute?"

She looks up, warm as ever. "Of course, honey. Have a seat. What's going on?"

I shift the coffee cup between my hands. "Joanne, I wanted to tell you myself. I got a promotion at the garage, which means I'll have to leave the rink. It wasn't an easy decision, but with everything changing, it's the right move for me.

She nods slowly, but I see the tension settle into her shoulders before she speaks. "I knew this was going to happen. When's your last day?"

She's nervous. They need someone to do my job. But, I'm not just going to abandon them. Not after everything they've done for my family.

My parents couldn't afford the extra training Nina needed to get to the level she's at now. She started late, almost fourteen when she laced up for the first time. Compared to the other skaters who've been on the ice since they were two, she's only been skating for nine years. That is a disadvantage in this sport.

But the rink sponsors Nina. That has been a huge help to my parents. They still scrape together what they can for Nikolai's coaching, but at least the rink covers the ice time, travel, and gear. It's a weight lifted. They don't talk about it, but I know they feel it.

"I don't need to leave any time soon," I tell her. "Find someone to replace me first."

The relief on Joanne's face is immediate. They don't need to struggle.

My parents should be able to relax, but I know they won't. Nationals is fast approaching and all three trainees are going. That means even more pressure, more sacrifices, more late nights spent figuring out how to make it all work.

I exhale a sigh of relief and head to the workshop, ready to set everything up before I cut the ice.

The sharp scrape of blades cuts through the quiet. The sound is off. Too much force, too deep an edge.

It makes me glance up.

That is when I see Valeria.

She looks different. Like there's something wrong.

There's something about the way she moves, the way she carries herself. She looks like she is barely holding it together. She looks too tight, too wound up.

She takes off into a jump, pulling in fast, her rotation sharp. For a second, I think she has it.

Then she lands. Wobbles. Puts her foot down.

My brow furrows, that's not like her. I haven't really taken the time to watch her skate before, we haven't even crossed paths before the party, though I'm not sure how. But from everything I've heard, and even witnessed, she's not the type to make that sort of mistake.

I see the flash of frustration, the sharp inhale, the clench of her jaw. She's pissed.

She circles back, resets, attacks the jump harder. Too hard. Her blade catches. She crashes.

The sound of her body hitting the ice makes my stomach tighten. That one had to hurt.

She gets up slowly, rolling her shoulders, pressing her lips together like she is willing herself not to react.

"Valeria," Nikolai's voice cracks through the air. Sharp. Unforgiving. "What the hell was that?"

She exhales hard, still shaking out her wrist. "I—"

"You can land a triple flip in your sleep," he snaps. "Why are you skating like an amateur?"

"I don't know," she fires back, her voice clipped, angry. "I have no idea what is wrong with me."

Nikolai steps closer to the boards, his eyes drilling into her. His tone is not just frustrated now. It is razor sharp.

"Then figure it out. Fast. Nationals are not months away anymore. They are weeks. You do not have time for this."

She doesn't respond. Just stands there, breathing hard, fists clenched.

"You're weak right now," he says, softer but somehow worse. "You are better than this."

I watch as her jaw tightens, her entire body locking up.

She storms off the ice without another word, shoving her guards on, shoulders rigid, spine straight.

Like if she keeps herself together physically, the rest won't crack.

I follow her to the locker room, grabbing her arm before she can disappear inside. "Hey, Valeria. Are you okay?"

She exhales sharply, ripping her arm free. "I'm fine."

She's not.

"Val—"

"Ethan, what do you want?" she snaps, turning on me, eyes flashing. Sharp. Defensive. Ready for a fight.

"I want to make sure you're okay after that fall."

She laughs, but it is bitter, cutting. "I said I'm fine."

"You're not."

She steps closer, shoulders squared, jaw tight, like she's daring me to challenge her. "I don't need you hovering. I don't need you checking on me. I don't need you acting like you give a damn about how I feel."

That pisses me off.

"You think I don't?" I fire back.

"I think it doesn't matter," she snaps. "I think I have more important things to focus on than whatever the hell this is."

Her breathing is sharp, fast, like she's holding back something bigger than this fight. I should walk away. I should let it go.

But I don't.

"You're running yourself into the ground."

"And?" She tilts her head, daring me to say it out loud.

"And it's going to destroy you."

Her jaw tightens. Her fists clench at her sides. For a second, I think she's going to shove me away again.

Then, her hands are on me.

She grabs my wrist. Hard. Her fingers wrap tight, her body tense, her breathing unsteady.

"Come with me," she says.

I hesitate. "Where are we going?"

She grabs my shirt. Her eyes flick to my mouth.

She leans in—just enough to let the tension sink into my skin, to let the heat between us stretch unbearably thin.

"You know what would make me feel better?" she murmurs.

A breath. A pause.

I swallow. "What?"

A smirk tugs at her lips, dark and reckless, but her eyes say something else. "Let's fuck."

And then she yanks me inside.

The argument still lingers in the air. Sharp. Heated. Unresolved.

She doesn't want to talk. She wants to forget.

And she wants to do it with me.

She yanks me forward, mouth crashing into mine. Hard. Desperate. Teeth, tongue, breath—nothing soft, nothing hesitant.

I growl against her lips, grabbing her hips, spinning her, pressing her against the locker before she can second-guess this. Her breath stutters at the impact.

She likes it.

Her hands move fast, tugging at my shirt, nails dragging over my abs, scraping along my obliques as she pulls me in. My hands are already at her leggings, shoving them down just enough, just so I can touch her.

Fuck. She's drenched.

Her fingers tighten in my hair, her body jerking when I slide my fingers through her slick folds. She's not waiting. She's not teasing.

She's rolling her hips, grinding down, chasing the friction, pushing harder, faster, until her breath is nothing but a sharp, uneven gasp.

I bite down on her jaw, dragging my lips to her ear. "This what you need?" My voice is rough, guttural.

She barely nods, one hand braced against the locker, the other fisting my shirt.

I don't wait.

I unfasten my jeans, free my cock, and lift her. Her thighs wrap around me, her core hot and wet against me, making my jaw clench.

I pause, grip tightening on her waist. "Val—"

She knows what I am asking.

"Pill," she gasps out, nails biting into my shoulders. "I'm on it."

That's all I need.

I thrust into her in one smooth stroke, her tight heat stretching around me, pulling me in, stealing my fucking breath.

She gasps, her back arching, legs locking tighter around my waist.

I freeze for half a second.

Then she moves.

Her hips roll, her body tight, desperate, clenching around my cock like she can't get close enough.

I slam into her, hard, fast, unrelenting. The metal lockers rattle with every thrust, her breath stutters, her nails drag down my back.

She holds on like she needs something to anchor her.

Or maybe she is the one drowning.

Her core squeezes around me, thighs trembling, muscles flexing, moans swallowed against my skin.

Fuck.

She's already close.

I feel it in the way her entire body locks, the way she shudders, the way she completely fucking falls apart around me.

That's all it takes.

I bury my face in her neck, teeth biting down, cock throbbing as I follow her over the edge.

I hold her there, panting, shaking, both of us wrecked.

She's still clinging to me, her fingers tangled in my hair.

Then she exhales and pushes lightly against my chest.

I already know what is coming.

She straightens her clothes, avoids my eyes. And then she walks away without a word.

Like this wasn't everything.

But it was.

And I can't fucking pretend otherwise.

I brace my hands against the locker, exhaling hard, trying to push past the way my body still feels her, the way my head is still spinning, the way none of this, none of her, is something I can shake off. My pulse is still hammering, my skin burning where she touched me, where she pulled me in, and yet, there's something heavier settling in my chest, something I can't ignore.

Because this wasn't just sex.

It wasn't just frustration or release or something we can both walk away from and pretend never happened.

It was her.

And if she thinks she can leave like nothing happened, like she isn't unraveling right in front of me, like I didn't just feel how much she needed that, needed me, then she doesn't know me at all. Which, to be fair, she doesn't, but I'm going to change that.

I drag a hand down my face, inhale deep, try to steady myself before I find her.

But I already know it won't help.

Because the second I step into the rink again, I see her.

She is sitting near the benches, tying her skates. Too fast. Too tight. Like she is trying to outrun something.

I sit beside her, still feeling the weight of what just happened, still hearing the sound of her breathing unevenly against my skin, still tasting her on my lips. But my voice is steady. "I know you're not eating, Val."

She freezes, just for a second. A split-second hesitation before she keeps tying, before she acts like she didn't hear me.

Then—"I am."

"Not enough."

She exhales sharply, shoulders tensing, already bracing for a fight. "I'm fine, Ethan."

I shake my head. "No, you're not."

She lets out a frustrated laugh, quick, sharp, humorless, like this conversation is just another thing she doesn't have time for. "Jesus. I don't need this from you."

"You don't need it from me," I say, watching as she pulls the laces so tight I know it has to hurt, "but you're going to hear it, anyway."

She scoffs, looking away. "I'm not at my optimal level."

My chest tightens. "What does that even mean?"

She looks at me then, and for a second, I swear I see something break in her expression. But she blinks, and it's gone. "I need to be lighter to jump better."

The words land like a gut punch. I shake my head. "No, you don't. You were stronger before."

She exhales, frustrated, like I don't get it. Like I never will.

"Why do you care?" she asks, voice quieter now, like she's not sure she even wants the answer.

I don't answer right away, because there are a hundred things I could say, and none of them feel big enough.

Because it's not just about skating. It's not just about the way she pushes herself to the edge of breaking every time she steps on the ice. It's about how I see her. How I've been seeing her. And how, no matter how much she keeps trying to push me out, I'm still here.

I exhale, rubbing a hand over my jaw. "Because it's you, Val. And I can't stand watching you do this to yourself."

She stills.

Her fingers tighten in the laces, knuckles going white, and for a second, she looks like she wants to run, like she wants to pretend she didn't hear me, like she's already thinking of the fastest way to shut this down.

"You don't mean that," she whispers, but it doesn't sound like a challenge. It sounds like a defense. Like she's daring me to prove her wrong.

I lean forward, forearms resting on my knees, my voice low, even. "Yeah, I do."

She looks at me, and this time, she doesn't blink it away. She just stares, like she doesn't know what to do with this. With me.

And for the first time, I think she's scared.

Her fingers curl in her lap, pressing into the fabric of her leggings, like she needs something to hold onto.

I exhale, lowering my voice. "Why did you pull me into that locker room, Val?"

She tenses. "I don't know."

I shake my head. "Bullshit. You know."

She clenches her jaw but doesn't say anything.

So, I keep going. "You were angry. You were frustrated. And you needed to forget. Why?"

Her eyes flicker, something flashing through them so fast I almost miss it. But I don't. She inhales sharply, looking away. "Because if I stop, I have to feel everything."

The silence is deafening.

The words hang there, heavy, real, like she wishes she could take them back.

But she can't.

And I won't let her.

I nod slowly, because I get it. She has spent her whole life focused, controlled, pushing everything else aside. Letting someone in? That's new.

"Then let's figure it out," I say.

She hesitates. One second. Two. Then, she exhales, and it's like something in her gives. "Okay," she says softly.

Not defiant. Not fighting.

Just a choice.

A choice to try.

A choice to let me in.

Nine
Valeria

WHAT DO I DO next?

I have *never* felt this way before. Not like this. Not with someone like him.

I like Ethan. More than I should, more than I know how to handle, if I'm being honest with myself.

It has always been me. Just me. I push myself. I fall. I get back up. I don't ask for help. I don't need anyone.

But Ethan isn't just anyone. And for the first time, I am starting to wonder what it would be like to let someone stay.

He watches me, silent and steady, not pushing, not demanding—just waiting.

I know he sees it. The fight in my head, the way I'm trying to make sense of this, of him, of what we are.

We've been honest with each other from the start. Brutally, painfully honest. Maybe that's why this feels different. Maybe that's why I should stop fighting it.

Better yet—maybe I should give myself a chance to be happy. I haven't had anything outside of the ice, I wouldn't even be friends with Nina if I didn't see her here.

I exhale, pulse kicking up, because I already know what I want to say. And that terrifies me. I wet my lips, my throat tight, forcing myself to look at him. *Say it. Say it before you talk yourself out of it.*

"I want to try this."

Ethan's brows lift slightly, but he doesn't look shocked. He looks like he was waiting for me to say it.

"With me?" His voice is steady, but there's a quiet kind of hope underneath.

I swallow hard. Saying it makes it real. "Yeah."

A long beat of silence follows my reluctant confession. My chest tightens and my hands curl into my lap, pressing against my thighs like I need something to hold onto.

Then, slowly, Ethan nods. "Okay."

That's it. No questions. No hesitation. He's choosing this, too.

I exhale, the tension in my chest loosening just a little, but something else settles there, something heavier, something real.

I don't know what comes next. I don't have all the answers.

But I want to figure it out.

NATIONALS ARE TWO WEEKS away. My program should feel perfect by now. Every jump should be second nature, every movement locked into my body like instinct. But something is wrong.

Technically, I have everything. I'm landing all my jumps, my spins don't travel, my footwork is sharp. But when I watch it back, it still feels... empty.

I've been seeing a dietitian to get the results I want the right way. I haven't told anyone. Not even Ethan.

It's not a secret. But I'm keeping it like one. I don't know why.

Maybe because if I say it out loud, he'll look at me like I'm fragile. Like I need saving. That's probably the worst thing he could do.

The rink is empty except for me. It has been for hours.

"What are you still doing here, Valeria? You've been here since this morning." I turn at the sound of Nikolai's voice. He stands by the boards, arms crossed, watching me like he already knows the answer.

"I just want to try something with my program, if that's okay."

He doesn't say anything at first, just exhales through his nose and gestures toward the ice. A silent go-ahead.

He's going to watch and tell me if this sucks.

I step back onto the ice, find my starting position and press my fingers into my sides.

The music starts, and I begin like I always do—controlled, precise, every step exactly where it should be. But this time, I let myself move.

My hands extend, fingers tracing shapes in the air, my body shifting in time with the melody. Not just steps and transitions. There's real emotion behind it.

I arch through my opening sequence, letting my head tip back, letting the music pull something out of me instead of just calculating the rhythm.

Stepping into my first turn, I soften my arms instead of holding them rigid. My fingertips brush over my collarbone before reaching upward, the movement smooth, like I am reaching for something just out of my grasp.

More breath. More space. Less force.

I step into my next jump, but instead of focusing only on height, I extend my free leg just a fraction longer, let my arms sweep out wider as I land. It's a small detail, something I would have dismissed before. But now, it feels right.

I move through the next section, not just skating but performing.

Not just counting beats. Not just preparing for the next jump. For once, I just let myself be in it.

The music fades, and I hold my final position longer than usual, letting the moment settle into my muscles before I straighten.

I exhale, pulse still steady from the routine, but my chest feels different—lighter.

For the first time in a long time, I felt it.

I turn toward Nikolai, bracing for his usual critique. A correction, a dismissal, another thing to fix.

But he's just standing there. Arms crossed, eyes locked on me like he is assessing something he has never seen before.

Silence. Then he nods once, it's small, but enough. "That," he says, voice even, measured in a way that makes my stomach tighten, "was incredible."

The words hit harder than any criticism ever has.

He steps closer, his gaze sharper now, assessing, weighing. "You have always been precise, always been powerful. But that? That was something else entirely." His expression shifts, something rare flashing in his eyes. "That was artistry."

I've spent years chasing his approval, perfecting every edge, every takeoff, every landing, but this is the first time he has looked at me like I did something more.

Something beyond technique.

Something beyond control.

Something real.

His voice lowers, quieter, but still firm. "Do you feel it now?"

I swallow, gripping the boards. "Yes."

He nods again, his mouth lifting in something that almost looks like satisfaction. "Good. Then do it again."

My body is still buzzing when I step off the ice, my muscles alive with something deeper than exhaustion. Not just from the movement, not just from the routine, but from the shift.

I untie my skates slowly, my fingers moving on autopilot, my mind still tangled in Nikolai's words.

That was artistry.

I roll my shoulders, stretch out my legs, but the tightness in my chest doesn't fade. It lingers, curling around my ribs, settling somewhere deep.

I should be thinking about my jumps, about my timing, about Nationals. I should be picking apart what went right, what I need to adjust, how to make it sharper.

But instead, all I can think about is how it felt. How it felt to just... let go.

I exhale, shaking out my limbs, forcing myself back into routine. Back into control.

Lacing up my sneakers, I tug on my sweatshirt, the fabric warm against my still-heated skin. The air inside the rink is heavy, thick with the energy I left on the ice.

The cold air outside hits fast, cutting through the left-over warmth still clinging to my skin, sending a sharp, electric jolt through my body. It feels almost like a reset, a shock to the system.

I barely register it before I hear his voice.

"Thought you'd be here." Ethan is leaning against the wall near the entrance, hands in his pockets, watching me like he has been waiting.

I open my mouth, but no words come. I don't know what I would even say. Before I can try, before I can ask why he's here, he nods toward the lot.

"Someone wants to see you." A second later, a familiar blur of energy appears, bundled up in a puffy jacket that makes her look half her size.

"Val!" Her voice is pure excitement, breathless and bright, cutting through the cold air like she couldn't possibly hold it in for another second.

I barely have time to react before CC is in front of me, bouncing on the balls of her feet, practically vibrating with enthusiasm.

Her eyes are wide, so wide, so full of something that makes my chest ache. "Your routine was so pretty!"

She grabs my hand, squeezing it like she needs me to feel how important this moment is.

"I saw you!" she says, her words tumbling over themselves. "I was watching the whole time, and it was so pretty. I want to skate like that someday!"

I blink at her, stunned. I've been coaching CC, teaching her mechanics, drilling her technique, making sure her foundation is solid. Together, we've been breaking down jumps, refining her edges, correcting her posture.

But she doesn't say she wants to jump like me. She says she wants to *skate* like me.

The realization hits deeper than I expect.

For a moment, I don't know how to respond. My first instinct is to correct her—to tell her she has a long way to go, that she's not ready yet, that I'm not ready yet.

But then, I catch the way she looks at me. And, for the first time, I don't push it away.

I kneel down, adjusting her scarf, my fingers moving instinctively, like I need to do something with my hands to process what is happening.

Ethan is watching us, standing just a step back, his presence steady, quiet, warm. He doesn't say anything, doesn't interrupt, just lets me have this moment.

I look back at CC, her excitement so pure, so certain.

"You already do," I tell her softly.

She tilts her head, her little nose scrunching.

I smile, something small but real. "You're going to be amazing, CC."

She beams. Completely believing me. And I realize—I believe it too.

When I stand up and meet Ethan's gaze, for a moment, neither of us speak. He just watches me, eyes searching, waiting, steady in a way that makes my chest feel too tight.

For once, I don't feel like running.

He exhales slowly, voice softer than I expect. "That was beautiful."

I know he isn't just talking about CC's excitement. He saw me out there. Saw the way I let myself move, the way I let the music pull me instead of forcing myself through every step. He saw what I felt, what I haven't allowed myself to feel in a very long time.

My pulse jumps, my breath catches, but I don't look away. I don't know what I'm supposed to say to that, so I don't say anything at all.

Ethan steps closer, slow and deliberate, like he's giving me time to stop him, to push him away, to run.

I don't.

His fingers brush against my cheek, barely there, a fleeting touch, but it lingers, his warmth sinking into my skin, grounding me in place. There's no urgency in his expression, no pressure—just patience, certainty, like he would wait as long as it takes.

Then he leans in, pressing his lips to mine.

The kiss is gentle, slow, unhurried, nothing like the last time we were tangled up in each other. There is no desperation here, no frustration—just the quiet weight of something real, something I can't run from anymore.

Just Ethan, steady as ever, letting me feel this in my own time.

Letting me choose it.

I exhale against his lips, my fingers curling slightly at my sides.

When he pulls back, he doesn't step away. His thumb grazes my cheek once before he drops his hand, like he's giving me space, but I don't think I need it.

He exhales, a small smirk tugging at the corner of his mouth. "Drew's throwing a party at his place."

I blink, still catching up, still feeling the warmth of his mouth against mine. "Drew?"

He nods. "Yeah. He's planning to propose to Nina and wants to have the engagement party right after." His voice is light, but the way he watches me is anything but. "Would you come with me?"

It's a simple question, one I should be able to answer without hesitation, but something about it makes my stomach flip.

Going with him means something. This isn't casual. It's not just a question about a party.

It's an invitation into his world.

I hesitate, just for a second, long enough to feel the weight of the choice settle into my bones.

A small smile tugs at my lips, barely there. "Yeah. I'll go."

Before Ethan can respond, CC gasps so loudly it startles me, her entire body vibrating with excitement. "Wait! Does this mean you're a couple now?"

I freeze. My mouth opens, but nothing comes out.

CC turns to Ethan, her eyes wide, bouncing on her toes like she can barely contain herself. "Are you and Val a couple?"

Ethan glances down at her, his smirk softening, something thoughtful flickering across his face. "Would you be okay with that?"

CC gasps again, even more dramatically this time, throwing her hands over her mouth like she just heard the most important news of her life. "Yes! That's the best news ever!"

Ethan chuckles, shaking his head as he looks back at me. His expression shifts, the teasing edge fading, something quieter, steadier settling in its place. His voice drops slightly, just enough that it feels like this moment belongs to us.

"What do you say, Val?" There's no pressure in his tone, no expectation, just the same quiet patience he has given me since the beginning. "Care to make this official?"

My breath catches. The old instinct kicks in—the one that tells me to deflect, to push this away before it becomes too much, before I let myself need something I don't know how to hold onto.

I hesitate, not because I don't want this.

Because I do. And that terrifies me.

I spent my entire life believing I didn't need anyone. That control was what mattered, that discipline would protect me from everything else.

Ethan breaks that apart just by standing here.

He didn't push when I shoved him against a locker and used him to forget. He didn't push when I tried to act like it meant nothing. He didn't even push when he saw me unraveling, when he called me out on what I was doing to myself.

He just stayed.

I think about the moments that led me here—not just the big ones, not just the arguments or the desperate touches, but the quiet ones. The way he looks at me like

I'm something worth seeing. The way he listens, even when I'm not saying anything. The way he never asks me to be anything other than what I am.

I think about how easy it would be to say no. To walk away before this turns into something I can't undo. But I don't want to.

I meet his gaze, my heart pounding, my fingers flexing at my sides before I step forward, closing the space between us. "Yeah."

The word settles between us, heavier than it should be, lighter than I expected.

I nod once, something solid and certain rooting in my chest. "Let's make it official."

CC lets out an ear-splitting cheer, jumping up and down, her excitement so pure, so overwhelming, that I can't help but laugh. Ethan just looks at me, his smile slow and certain, not cocky, not triumphant.

Just happy.

Ten
Valeria

"YOU LOOK BEAUTIFUL, HONEY," Mom says, her voice warm.

"Thank you, Mom," I reply, a little shy. I've heard it plenty before, but I've never liked being the center of attention.

I glance at my reflection. Other than the night of the party, I don't usually dress up.

Full-circle moment, honestly.

The dress is simple but elegant—a deep navy, fitted at the waist, with thin straps that leave my shoulders bare. The fabric is smooth, hugging my frame without feeling constricting. Not too flashy, not too much. Just enough.

My hair is down, something I rarely let happen. The soft waves fall over my shoulders in stark contrast to the usual tight ponytail or bun.

I like this side of myself. More relaxed. Lighter. Happier.

That's when it hits me—Ethan makes me happy. Maybe he has since the first night I met him. There's something electric about him, something effortless and steady.

I'm glad I get to know him like this, without pressure, without rushing into something we can't define yet. We haven't put any labels on us, haven't said what we are. We just... exist together. And until his wife signs the divorce papers, that's all I'm willing to do.

The doorbell rings, and I take a steadying breath before heading downstairs, my heels quiet against the hardwood.

As I reach the bottom step, I hear my dad's voice.

"So, how's the garage treating you?"

"Busy," Ethan replies, his tone easy, familiar, like he's not just answering to impress him but actually enjoying the conversation. "Drew's been talking my ear off about upgrading some of the lifts. Swears it'll change our lives."

Dad chuckles. "He sounds like the type if he can't re-build it, he'll try to make it better."

Ethan huffs out a quiet laugh. "Yeah, well, he's got me pulling more hours than I planned, but I guess I can't complain. I like working with my hands."

There's nothing forced about it. Just two men talking, like they've known each other longer than they actually have. Like my dad already likes him.

And then—Ethan looks at me.

It's not just a glance. It's the kind of look that makes my stomach dip, the kind that sends something electric through my veins, sharp and unshakable.

Ethan's gaze drags over me, slow, deliberate, like he's committing every detail to memory. Like he's seeing me for the first time—but also like he already knew exactly what he would find.

And maybe I should have expected him to look good, but I didn't expect... this.

He's clean-shaven, his jaw sharper under the dim light. His dark hair is styled just enough to look effortless but not careless. He's wearing a fitted button-down, the sleeves rolled up slightly at his forearms, the deep blue fabric stretching over broad shoulders.

It's different from his usual—no grease stains, no worn flannel, no work boots. And I can't stop looking.

His lips part slightly, but he doesn't say anything at first. He doesn't have to. Because I feel it. Everywhere.

My breath catches, the warmth of his attention settling over me in a way I don't know what to do with.

Dad clears his throat, breaking whatever moment we were locked in.

Ethan blinks, like he's just remembered we're not alone.

"You clean up nice," he finally says, voice low, eyes still holding onto something I can't name.

I should say something back, but I don't trust my voice just yet.

I hear Ethan chuckle.

"You ready to go?" he asks, and it's casual, but there's something in his voice that lingers, something heavier than the words.

"Yeah," I say, exhaling quietly.

I give my mom a hug and kiss my dad on the cheek, feeling a familiar warmth settle in my chest.

Then, I turn to Ethan. Without thinking, I reach for his hand. His fingers curl around mine, warm, steady, grounding.

And then—he rubs his thumb along my skin. Slow. Deliberate. Like he isn't just holding my hand but holding me in place.

A breath I didn't realize I was holding slips out, my body instantly relaxing, but it's more than that. I feel... held. Not just touched. Not just steadied. But held.

The kind of touch that says I've got you, without needing the words.

This time, when I walk into Drew's house it's different.

I'm not showing up alone. I'm not showing up because I feel obligated, because Nina begged me, because it's easier to say yes than to argue.

I want to be here.

I want to celebrate my friend, to stand beside her on one of the happiest nights of her life. I've come so far from the person who used to avoid things like this. I was forced to go to the party that night, but now? Now, I'm choosing this.

We walk in, hand in hand, and as the crowd settles, Ethan moves behind me, wrapping his arms around my waist, his chest solid against my back.

He leans down, his lips brushing my ear. A whisper, just for me. "I hear a car door closing. I think they're coming in."

I nod slightly, eyes flicking over the room, taking in the faces around us. This is family.

Ethan's parents are here. Ryan, CC. Close friends, familiar faces. Even Zara.

I glance toward the far wall and spot Ryan standing next to her. Close and relaxed, their heads tilt toward each other, their conversation quiet, intimate.

Ethan had mentioned Ryan asked her out. I would have never guessed she'd said yes. She's as dedicated to skating as I am, neither of us has ever had much of a social life.

I don't know why I watch them for a second longer than I should.

Maybe because it's strange, watching something begin in real time. Seeing two people shift from possibility into something tangible and real.

Or maybe because I know exactly how that feels.

The front door swings open, and Nina steps inside, Drew right behind her.

"Surprise!" we all call out.

Nina laughs—bright, open, overflowing with joy.

She runs to her parents first, throwing her arms around them, her excitement radiating so strongly that the whole room seems to glow with her.

She looks adorable, as always. A white dress, soft and flowy, cinched at the waist, catching the light with a subtle shimmer. Elegant, but effortless. Playful, but still refined. Very Nina.

And, of course, she's wearing bright pink heels.

Before she can come over, CC bolts toward her, her little boots tapping against the floor as she yells out in pure excitement.

"Aunt Nina! Hi!"

Nina turns just in time, grinning as she bends down to catch CC in a hug. "Hey, little bug!" she says, ruffling CC's hair.

CC pulls back, still bouncing. "Daddy brought Valeria!"

Ethan groans lightly, rubbing a hand over his face. "CC..."

CC ignores him entirely.

Nina's eyes flick up to me, and her entire expression brightens.

"I see." She winks at Ethan, then stands up, smoothing out her dress. "I'm going to go say hi."

I watch as she makes her way over to us, her excitement still buzzing in the air around her. She wraps Ethan in a hug first, squeezing him tight before turning to me. "Val! I'm so glad you're here!"

"Congratulations!" I say, feeling myself smile for her. "Can I see the ring?"

She practically shoves her hand toward me. Her fingers tremble slightly, like she's still trying to believe this is real.

The ring is... perfect. A delicate yet stunning vintage design, the center stone a deep sapphire instead of a diamond, flanked by tiny diamonds on either side. Elegant but bold. Classic, but uniquely hers.

It looks exactly like something Drew would pick. Something meant just for her.

"Let's start the party!" Drew calls, and the room bursts into motion.

Music pulses through the speakers, drinks are poured, conversation swells into an easy, lively rhythm. Laughter spills through the air, and warmth fills the space. Everything about the moment feels effortless, unshaken, untouched by anything outside of it.

But then—something shifts.

It's subtle at first, just a feeling. Like the air has thickened, like an unseen presence has settled into the space. I wouldn't have noticed it right away, not if Ethan hadn't gone still beside me.

His entire body tenses.

His fingers tighten around his drink, his posture losing its relaxed ease in an instant. The second I glance up at him, I see it. His jaw is locked, his body braced like he's waiting for impact.

Something's wrong.

I follow his gaze toward the entrance.

A woman stands just inside the doorway, watching the room like she's taking inventory. Like she's deciding where she belongs in it.

She's impossible to miss.

Platinum blonde hair, sleek and sharp against the dark liner smudged around striking green eyes. Her makeup is bold, dramatic, designed to draw attention, and from the way she carries herself, I can already tell that's exactly what she's used to.

Her dress is short. Tight. Intentionally edgy. Fishnet stockings disappear into impossibly high heels that somehow make her presence feel even more imposing. She looks like she walked straight off a stage and into this room without a second thought, like she belongs anywhere she decides to stand.

And right now, she's standing in a room full of people who weren't expecting her.

Something in my stomach twists. I don't know who she is. But the energy in the room shifts around her, the laughter thinning, the ease cracking at the edges.

A small voice cuts through the noise, piercing in its innocence. "Mommy?"

I barely have time to register the word before CC stiffens in Ethan's arms, her little hands fisting into his shirt.

Ethan's grip tightens around her. He exhales, slow, controlled. But I don't miss the way his shoulders go rigid, his knuckles whitening against the glass in his hand.

His voice is quieter than I expect when he finally speaks. "Margo."

The name lands like a dropped glass, shattering whatever celebration existed in the room just moments ago.

Ethan looks at her like she's a collision waiting to happen—I already know enough.

She wasn't invited.

And she isn't here to celebrate.

Eleven

Valeria

MARGO STEPS INSIDE THE house, and the world freezes. Her heels click against the floor, slicing through the warmth of the party like a knife.

CC stiffens in Ethan's arms, her tiny fingers gripping his shirt tighter, like she wants to disappear.

Margo's eyes land on her daughter first, lips curving into something too sharp to be a real smile. "Well, hello, my child." Her voice drips with mock sweetness. "Aren't you excited to see me?"

CC presses her face into Ethan's chest, shrinking. "Daddy..."

Margo tilts her head, smirk widening. "No hug? Nothing?"

Ethan's grip tightens. "Stop, Margo. Just stop."

She barely acknowledges him. Her attention shifts—locking onto me.

"I see my husband and daughter aren't happy to see me." Her voice is smooth, practiced, razor-sharp. "Probably because of you."

Before I can move, before I can even breathe—she slaps me. Hard.

The force jerks my head sideways, heat exploding across my cheek.

Gasps ripple through the room.

The entire party falls into stunned silence. My ears ring. My skin burns. Humiliation sinks in before the pain even registers.

Ethan's voice is lethal. "Margo." He tucks CC into his shoulder more, keeping her from seeing whatever is about to happen.

Margo just smiles, satisfied and amused, like she just proved a point.

She leans in, voice dropping just enough for only me to hear.

"Is that how you get ahead, Valeria?" The words drip from her lips, slow, cruel. "By fucking someone that isn't yours? Or by sleeping your way to the top?"

The room doesn't breathe. I don't move. Because if the slap humiliated me, this destroys me. Even though I know it's not true. Ethan is the only person I've ever slept with, I've worked hard for everything I have, but it still hurts.

The weight of her words presses down, suffocating, wrapping around my ribs, curling around my throat. My cheek still stings, but it's nothing compared to the way my stomach twists, the way I feel every single set of eyes locked on me, watching, waiting.

Hannah walks up behind us, taking CC from Ethan's arms as he moves beside me, his entire body coiled, voice controlled but razor-sharp. "Margo, that's enough."

She doesn't look at him. Her focus stays on me, gaze dragging over me like she's sizing up something cheap and disposable. "She really thinks she belongs here, doesn't she?"

Ethan clenches his fists. "Don't do this."

Margo ignores him, her voice carrying through the stunned silence. "She really thinks spreading her legs for my husband gets her a place at this table?"

The air thickens. The whispers start. My stomach twists.

Ethan takes a step forward, jaw tight. "You don't get to talk about her like that."

Margo smirks. "Why not? It's the truth, isn't it?" She turns toward the crowd, feeding off the attention, the power shift. "Tell me, is that how it works now? Sleep with the right man, and suddenly your family? In case you forgot, *I'm* his wife."

Ethan moves again, but Nina steps in first.

"Almost ex-wife," Nina corrects, voice steady, slicing through the tension like a blade. "You just need to sign."

Margo whips toward her. "Stay out of this, Nina."

Nina doesn't flinch. "Oh, honey, this is my brother, my niece, my family. I am in this."

Drew shakes his head. "No one invited you, Margo. You're embarrassing yourself."

Ryan lets out an unimpressed breath. "Nothing new there."

Margo's hands clench into fists, her control slipping. She turns toward Ethan, voice rising. "You don't know a damn thing about what I've been through."

Grant steps forward, voice calm but unshakable. "Unless something dramatic has happened in the *year* since you left your daughter, we all know what you've 'been through'."

Margo whips toward him, but before she can fire back, Hannah steps in. "You don't just get to show up here and act like nothing happened."

Margo exhales sharply, shaking her head, hands flaring out. "Nothing happened? I was out there working. Making something of myself while Ethan played single father and let some skater girl step into my place."

She spins back to me, eyes burning. "Did you enjoy it? Sliding into my life? Sleeping in my husband's bed? Playing mommy to my daughter?"

I don't flinch. But I feel it.

"You really think he'll keep you?" she murmurs. "You think you belong here?"

The voices around us swell, colliding.

Ethan snaps, stepping in front of me. "You're the one who walked away, Margo!"

"You don't get to play the victim when you're the one who left!" Nina fires back.

Drew's voice cuts through. "This isn't about Valeria. This is about you not wanting to lose."

Margo's voice rises. "I didn't lose! This is my family! My husband!"

Grant's voice booms, final and unwavering. "Not anymore."

Hannah steps forward. "Enough, Margo."

The shouting continues, voices overlapping. But I don't hear it anymore.

Because I hear something else.

A small, broken sob. The kind that cuts through everything. CC is crying.

Her small body trembles in Hannah's arms, fingers curled tightly into her shirt, pressing into her grandmother like she's trying to disappear.

And suddenly, nothing else matters.

I move without thinking, reaching for her. Hannah hesitates for only a second before letting me take her. The moment she's in my arms, her little hands grip my dress, her face pressing into my shoulder, her whole body shaking with quiet sniffles.

I whisper, my voice steady even though my heart is racing. "It's okay, baby. You're okay."

She doesn't lift her head, doesn't let go, just burrows deeper, holding on like I'm the only thing keeping her safe.

Ethan is still beside me, still tense, radiating barely contained rage.

But Margo moves. Her heels click against the floor. She reaches for CC.

"Let go of my daughter." Her voice is sharp, I can see she's trying to maintain control, but she's becoming more and more unhinged.

CC whimpers, her tiny frame pressing deeper into me, shaking her head.

Ethan steps forward, voice dark. "Margo, don't."

She doesn't listen. She grabs CC's arm—too hard. CC cries out in pain and fear.

My head snaps down and I see it. Margo's nails digging into CC's skin.

Something inside me ignites.

I rip CC away, stepping back, arms tightening protectively. My voice isn't loud. It isn't a scream. It's a growl. A warning. A promise. "Do not. Touch. Her."

Ethan moves between us, voice like steel. "You need to leave."

Margo doesn't back down. She turns on me, eyes burning with resentment, sharp and unforgiving. Her gaze doesn't just land on me—it *cuts* through me, piercing into every insecurity I refuse to acknowledge.

"This is your fault," she spits, her voice dripping with accusation, feeding off the chaos she created.

CC whimpers against me, her tiny frame trembling, fingers curling tighter into my dress like she's trying to disappear. I hold her closer, arms tightening protectively, but Margo keeps going, her voice rising, her fury unchecked. "You turned my family against me. You took my place. You think you belong here?"

Ethan moves between us, shoulders squared, his voice low and firm, leaving no room for argument. "I said, you need to leave."

The tension thickens, pressing against my ribs, making it harder to breathe. Margo's chest rises and falls too fast, her hands still clenched into fists, her jaw set like she refuses to be the one who backs down. But then her eyes flick to CC, a flicker of something crossing her face—anger, regret, something twisted and bitter that she refuses to let go of.

Hannah steps forward, voice gentle but unwavering. "Come here, sweetheart."

CC hesitates, her grip tightening one last time, her small fingers trembling against the fabric of my dress. My arms ache at the thought of letting her go, but I press a kiss to the top of her head.

Slowly, hesitantly, she loosens her grip, fingers slipping away as I carefully pass her back to Hannah. The loss is immediate, the warmth of her small body gone in an instant, leaving behind an emptiness that settles deep in my chest. Grant moves beside them, his silent presence reassuring, watchful, a quiet force ensuring that Margo doesn't try anything else.

But I barely register it.

Because Ethan is already gripping Margo's arm, pulling her toward the door with the same restrained fury that has been simmering beneath his skin since she walked in the door. She stumbles slightly in her heels, but she doesn't resist as hard this time, as if she finally understands that she has lost control of the moment. She whips her head back, one last glance toward CC, but her daughter doesn't even look at her.

The door slams shut behind them, the sound reverberating through the house like the final nail in what I should have known was temporary.

The party doesn't recover. Conversations don't immediately start up again. People shift awkwardly, whispering behind hands, stealing glances at me, at the place where Ethan and Margo just stood, at CC tucked safely into her grandmother's arms. The warmth that filled the house earlier is gone, the celebration drained from the air, replaced with a thick, suffocating weight that no one wants to be the first to acknowledge.

I don't move. I don't speak. Because I know exactly what just happened.

Margo didn't just come here to make a scene. She didn't just come back to see CC. She came back for Ethan.

And she wants her family back.

That realization settles deep, twisting through my ribs, pressing down on me in a way that feels inescapable. I feel it in my bones, in the way my fingers curl into my palms, in the way my chest tightens like it's bracing for impact.

I don't belong here.

I don't belong in the middle of whatever unfinished mess still exists between Ethan and the life he had before me. I don't belong standing in this house, surrounded by a family that has existed long before I ever stepped into it.

I have Nationals to win.

I have a career, a future, a dream I have spent my entire life chasing, one that has never included anything beyond the ice.

And whatever this was—me and Ethan, the thing we were building, the thing I let myself believe could be real—was never meant to last.

It's already over.

I turn to leave, my body moving before my mind fully catches up.

I pull out my phone, my fingers hovering over the screen. Mom? An Uber? I'm not sure, but I need to get out of here. Nina's voice cuts through the thick silence, stopping me in my tracks. "Val."

I don't want to look at her, don't want to see whatever concern is written across her face, don't want to let her sympathy pull me back into something I've already decided to walk away from. But when she reaches out, her fingers brushing against my wrist, I pause just enough to feel the warmth of her touch.

"It's going to be okay," she says softly, like she believes it.

I wish I could believe it too.

But I don't.

So I don't answer.

Instead, I pull my wrist free from her grasp, step away from the wreckage left behind, and walk out the door.

Twelve
Ethan

I CALL VALERIA AGAIN. It goes straight to voicemail. She blocked me. I can't blame her. My life is a mess—a ridiculous, spiraling mess, and it's only getting worse.

Margo's return wrecked everything. I rejected her. Told her to sign the papers, told her we had nothing left to talk about, that if she needed to communicate, she could go through Ryan. She didn't take it well.

Now she wants time with CC, and maybe she should get it—but only if CC wants to. For now, my parents are supervising their visits. It seemed like the best option until I heard CC start crying.

I shift on the couch, turning toward her, concern tightening in my chest. "Are you okay, sweetheart?"

She sniffs, wiping at her eyes with the sleeve of her pajama top. "I don't wanna see Mommy."

The words stop me cold.

I expected hesitation. Maybe some fear. But not this.

I keep my voice gentle, careful. "Why not, honey?"

Her small hands twist in her lap, fingers tangling together, like she's trying to hold something in. For a long moment, she doesn't say anything. Then, in a voice barely above a whisper, "She doesn't like me."

A slow, sinking dread spreads through my chest, wrapping tight around my ribs. I grip the couch, trying to process what she just said, trying to figure out how to fix something I don't even understand yet.

I tuck a curl behind her ear, forcing my voice to stay steady. "Sweetheart, what do you mean?"

CC sniffs again, looking down as she picks at a loose thread in her pants. "She's only nice when people are watching. When it's just us... she doesn't care."

My stomach twists. I clear my throat, swallowing back the anger already simmering beneath my skin. "Baby, tell me what happened."

She hesitates, shifting in place, her little shoulders curling inward. "She forgets things, Daddy."

I exhale slowly. "What kind of things?"

She shrugs, but it's not careless—it's defeated. "She forgot my birthday."

A sharp, cold weight settles in my stomach.

"She didn't even know how old I was," CC murmurs, voice small, like she's embarrassed to even say it out loud. "Grandma told her. And then she said happy birthday. But she didn't mean it."

I don't say anything because I don't trust myself to speak.

"She forgets my favorite color, too," CC adds after a moment, her voice barely above a whisper. "It's pink, Daddy. It's always been pink."

She shouldn't have to explain that. She shouldn't have to remind her own mother.

But then she exhales sharply, like she's been holding something in, like the words have been sitting on her tongue for too long. "She says I talk too much." I still. "She says I ask too many questions. That I whine. That I should stop being so loud."

A deep, burning rage coils inside me, tightening with every word.

"She says I act like a baby," CC continues, her voice wobbling. "I try to be good. I try really hard. But she still gets mad."

I inhale carefully, keeping my voice soft, even as my hands clench into fists. "How does she get mad, baby?"

"She sighs a lot. Like I'm annoying. And she rolls her eyes. And..." CC's voice drops to a whisper. "She yells sometimes."

I fight every instinct to react, to let the fury clawing up my throat break free, to stand up and destroy whatever control Margo still thinks she has. Instead, I force my voice to stay even. "Did she ever... hurt you?"

CC shakes her head quickly. "No. Not like that."

Relief should come. It doesn't.

"She just... stops listening," CC whispers. "She looks at her phone. She walks away. Sometimes she acts like I'm not even there."

I can't breathe. I should've known. I should have seen it.

"Why didn't you tell me?" I ask, voice barely above a whisper.

She hesitates, and when she finally speaks, her words are so soft, so fragile, I almost don't hear them. "Because I thought you were happy."

The breath leaves my lungs.

She thought I was happy with Margo. Until the day she walked out and didn't look back. That if she told me—if she admitted how she felt—she would ruin that for me.

My arms tighten around her, pressing a kiss to the top of her head, my voice low but firm. "Listen to me."

She sniffles, curling closer into my chest.

"You don't have to see her if you don't want to. Okay?"

She doesn't answer at first. Then, barely above a whisper, "But she's my mom."

The ache in her voice is unbearable.

I close my eyes, swallowing hard. "I know, baby. But a mom is supposed to make you feel safe. A mom is supposed to love you, take care of you. If she's not doing that, then you don't have to see her just because she's your mom."

CC doesn't say anything for a long moment. Then, finally, she exhales, her small shoulders sagging as the tension drains from her tiny frame. "I wanna go to bed, Daddy."

I kiss her hair. "Okay, baby. Let's get you tucked in."

I walk her to her room, pulling the covers up around her, smoothing a hand over her back. But as I step out of her room and close the door, a slow, burning anger spreads through my chest.

Margo doesn't get to do this to her.

She doesn't get to waltz back in, pick CC up like a trophy she abandoned, and expect her to shine.

She doesn't get to keep doing this. She sure as hell doesn't get to win.

I take out my phone to call my parents, but the doorbell rings. I sigh, running a hand over my face, hoping to God it isn't Margo.

My next sigh is one of relief as I see Nina, Drew, Ryan, and my parents. It takes a second, but there's two additional people behind them; Ana Lucia and Emilio Blaze.

Wordlessly, I step aside, letting them in, and shut the door behind us.

Emilio clears his throat, his expression tense as he holds up his phone. "We're not here for a good reason."

My stomach sinks.

On the screen—Margo. Sitting in my parents' house, staring into the camera.

CC inhales sharply beside me, her little voice barely a whisper. "Oh no..."

I press play.

She inhales shakily, then lets out a slow, measured breath, staring directly into the camera.

"I wasn't going to do this." Her voice wavers, but there's steel beneath the vulnerability. "But I can't sit back and let people keep worshiping someone who doesn't deserve it. Someone who destroyed my family."

A pause. A perfect, calculated pause.

"A few months ago, I was on tour." She exhales sharply. "A tour Ethan knew about, supported, and encouraged. It wasn't a surprise. It wasn't me abandoning my family. It was my career—the same way skating is for Valeria Blaze."

She leans forward, voice thick with resentment. "I was eighteen when I got pregnant. Fresh out of high school. I gave up everything for my family. I stayed. I put my dreams on hold. And how did Ethan repay me?"

Her voice hardens, ice creeping into every word. "By replacing me the second I left."

She wipes at her eyes, shaking her head. "And now? The world worships her. The golden girl of figure skating. But let's be real—do you really think she got here on skill alone?"

She lets the question hang.

"How many women lose their opportunities the second they get pregnant? But Valeria? She didn't have to choose. She just took what wasn't hers."

Her gaze sharpens.

"Sponsors. Fans. Companies backing Valeria Blaze—you're standing behind a homewrecker. A woman who slept her way to the top."

The video cuts to black.

I tighten my grip on Emilio's phone, my pulse hammering as I scan the headlines and comments.

Valeria Blaze: The Ice Queen Who Slept Her Way to the Top?

Major Sponsors Pull Support Following Margo Valentine's Explosive Video

"She doesn't deserve to compete."

"Knew she was too perfect. Fake bitch."

"Drop her from competing for Team USA. She's a disgrace."

The phone pings again with a statement from Valeria.

I have dedicated my entire life to this sport. Every success I've had is because of discipline, sacrifice, and relentless hard work. The accusations being made about me are false, and I refuse to let them overshadow what truly matters—my performance on the ice.

My personal life has never been, and will never be, a factor in my career. I will not engage in baseless rumors or let them distract me from my goals.

I will be at Nationals. I will be ready. My focus remains on my training, my performance, and my future.

—Valeria Blaze

I grip the phone so hard his knuckles turn white.

Ryan sighs, rubbing his temple. "I'm sorry, man... but Margo just filed for full custody."

"What?"

CC screams. "No! Daddy, no! Don't let her take me!"

I pull her into his arms. "Never, sweetie. But I think you need to tell Uncle Ryan what you told me about your mom."

She looks at me, clearly terrified, but I just nod. I will protect her at all costs.

Silence crashes down over the room, thick and suffocating, wrapping around each of us like a vice. The only sound is CC's shaky breaths, her little fingers clutching my shirt like I'm the only thing keeping her grounded.

Nina is the first to move, dropping into a crouch so she's eye level with CC. Her voice is gentle, but her eyes burn with fury. "Sweetheart, you don't have to be scared. No one—no one—is ever going to let her take you." She brushes a stray curl from CC's damp cheek, her hand trembling slightly.

Drew exhales hard, running a hand through his hair, looking like he's barely keeping his temper in check. "What the hell is wrong with her?" His voice is sharp, his usual easygoing nature completely gone. "She walks away for months, and now she thinks she deserves custody?" He shakes his head, his jaw locked. "Not happening."

Ryan doesn't move, doesn't blink, just crosses his arms, his expression unreadable. But when he speaks, his voice is low and sure. "She won't win." His gaze flicks to CC, softening for only a second. "A judge won't grant her full custody."

CC sniffs hard, trying to stay brave, but her grip on me tightens. "I don't wanna go with her," she whispers. "Please don't make me."

Mom reaches out, stroking CC's hair, her touch as light as her voice. "Baby, no one is going to make you do anything you don't want to do." Her words are calm, but there's a quiet storm behind them, her free hand gripping Dad's so tight her knuckles are white.

My father finally speaks, his voice carrying the kind of weight that makes everyone in the room listen. "She left," he says simply, his words deliberate, unwavering. "A parent doesn't do that. A real parent doesn't come back just to take something that was never theirs to begin with." His jaw tightens, and when he speaks again, his voice is final. "She is never getting her back."

A sharp gasp cuts through the silence.

I swallow hard and press a kiss to the top of CC's head, my voice steady even though my pulse is hammering in my chest. "Never, sweetie. I will never let her take you."

CC trembles against me, but she nods, just barely, like she believes me.

And I swear, I will do whatever it takes to make damn sure I don't break that promise.

Thirteen
Valeria

NATURALS. THE FINAL TEST. The moment that decides everything.

I roll my shoulders, breathing deep, shaking out my limbs. My body is ready, my muscles coiled, but my mind is loud. The arena hums with restless energy. Cameras flash. Voices echo. The weight of expectation presses down, thick and suffocating.

Somewhere, the commentators are speculating—Did the scandal get to her? Did she crack under pressure? Is she still the skater she was before all of this?

I shut them out. I'm here to win.

I glance toward the boards, toward the stands, searching for something—someone.

But the lights are too bright. The crowd is a sea of faces, blurring together, too many at once. I can't pick anyone out.

It doesn't matter. I don't need to see anyone. I know my parents are in the crowd, despite their busy lives, they've never missed a performance.

I need to skate.

The music begins, and I let my training take over. I push off, my blades carving into the ice, steady, controlled. The noise fades. The crowd dissolves. The cameras, the judges, the weight of expectation—none of it exists.

There is only this.

My movements are fluid, exact, every step hitting where it should. Not too much. Not too little. Just enough.

I push into my first combination—triple lutz, triple toe. Knees bend, body coils, and I launch, rotating fast, my core locked tight. The landing is clean, absorbed into the next transition.

No reaction. No hesitation. I keep moving.

The choreography sequence should feel effortless. It doesn't. The ice feels harder beneath my skates, my limbs tighter than usual, my breath shallower. I push through it.

Deep edges, sharp transitions, arms extending just enough to match the music. Not because I feel it—because I command it.

I prepare for my next combination—triple flip, double toe, double loop.

My body snaps into position in the flip, my skates touch down, for only a second, my weight feels too far back. A flicker of doubt. A fraction of hesitation.

I adjust instantly, flowing straight into the next jump.

It's fine. It's all fine.

But the fight is there.

I don't let it shake me. I don't let it rattle my control. I absorb the moment, I shift, I own every movement.

One final jump. Triple loop.

I step into it, push off strong, rotating effortlessly. The landing is clean, absorbed into the ice like it was always meant to be.

I coil in, the world blurring as I increase my speed. Faster, tighter, deliberate. Then, for the final extension, I extend, arms reaching outward, chin lifting—a flawless finish.

Silence.

A breath.

Cheers crash through the air, the roar of the crowd swelling, deafening. The energy pulses around me, vibrating through the ice, through my chest, through my bones.

Nikolai is waiting for me, eyes bright, his expression full of something rare—pride.

"That was brilliant!" He grabs my shoulders, squeezing. "You did it!"

I shake my head. "I can do better."

His grip tightens. "Stop that, Valeria. Accept your accomplishments. Accept your wins."

I exhale sharply, my pulse still pounding in my ears. "You don't even know if I won."

He huffs, like it's obvious. "You are winning."

I want to believe him. I really do.

I glance toward the stands, searching for my parents, for Grant and Hannah. They're there, standing, cheering, their expressions proud. But it still feels... distant. Like I haven't let it hit me yet.

I inhale slowly, trying to shake the residual energy still buzzing in my limbs. I should feel triumphant. Overwhelmed. Something.

Instead, I just feel... empty.

The competition is over. And suddenly, all I can think about is Ethan.

The music starts, and immediately, I see the difference between my style and Nina's. She doesn't attack the ice. She invites it in.

Where I cut through the rink with power, she moves like the music belongs to her. There's no force, no sharp edges—just breath, just glide, just something effortless in the way she lets herself be part of the performance.

She doesn't skate to hit every beat. She skates to feel it.

Her arms extend, fingers tracing unseen lines in the air, every movement deliberate, but never forced. Where my movements are clean and exact, hers are soft, expressive, open. Her face changes with the music, her body leans into every note, and for a moment, I swear I almost forget I'm watching a competition.

She's not just performing. She's telling a story.

She moves through the footwork sequence, her blade carving smooth, flowing arcs, her weight shifting effortlessly between edges. She's light, floating across the ice like she's not bound by gravity the way the rest of us are.

Her step sequence is hypnotic—deep edges, fluid turns, arms drifting seamlessly through each motion. It's mesmerizing. Every gesture, every glance, every breath seems like it belongs in the music.

The jumps come, but they don't define the program. They don't own the routine the way they do in mine.

They're woven in, almost secondary to the performance itself.

I'm not watching technique. I'm watching Nina.

And for the first time, I wonder if that's what I've been missing.

Her final spin unravels like a ribbon, slow and controlled before extending into her finishing pose—arms reaching toward the sky, a smile breaking across her face, the last note lingering in the air.

She skates off, her expression glowing, her joy undeniable. Drew is already reaching for her, pulling her into a hug before she even catches her breath.

It wasn't the most difficult program. It wasn't packed with the hardest jumps. But it was Nina. And it was unforgettable.

She looks to the monitors, waiting for her scores. The numbers flash. The crowd roars yet again. It's incredible. Her highest score yet.

Nina lets out a joyful laugh, practically throwing herself into Drew's arms, kissing him before hugging her parents. She's glowing, soaking in every moment, letting herself celebrate.

She deserves this.

I should be celebrating too. I should feel something. But my eyes scan the crowd, searching for someone who isn't here. I feel the absence of him like a weight in my chest, heavier than it should be, heavier than I want it to be.

Nina must notice, because she turns, catches me staring. Without waiting for an invitation, she comes over to me, arms crossed, watching me carefully. "He couldn't come."

I frown, my stomach twisting. "What?"

"He wanted to. He was supposed to." She exhales, rubbing a hand over her face. "But... Margo filed for full custody."

The words hit like a slap. My breath catches. "What?"

"Yeah," she nods, her voice tight. "Court hearings, meetings with Ryan—he has to stay with CC."

I stare at her, my heart hammering, my chest suddenly too tight.

She studies my reaction, then tilts her head. "He makes the same face you are now."

I swallow hard. "I don't—"

"I know you miss him," she cuts in, and something in her voice shifts. Softer. Sure.

I shake my head, but it's weak. "It doesn't matter."

"It does."

She steps closer, her eyes locked onto mine, unshaken. "Val, I don't think you understand something."

My voice is hoarse. "What?"

She exhales, like she can't believe she has to spell it out. "You're it for him."

My stomach clenches.

"He loves you, Val," she says simply, no hesitation, no doubt. "I've never seen him look at anyone the way he looks at you. Not even Margo."

I stiffen at the name, but Nina doesn't stop.

"I used to think my brother was just... done with love after everything she put him through. That he'd never let himself feel anything for someone again."

She gives a small, humorless laugh. "And then you walked into his life."

I press my lips together, my hands curling into fists at my sides.

"I've watched him, you know?" Nina's voice is almost amused, almost fond. "Every time you're in the room, he's

146

tuned into you. Even when you're not talking. Even when you're across the rink, not even looking at him, not even thinking about him—he's always thinking about you." She shakes her head. "I swear, Val, I've never seen my brother like this."

I drop my gaze, my pulse loud in my ears. "It's complicated, Nina."

"No," she says, her voice firm. "It was complicated. Before. When Margo was lurking, when you were running, when you both pretended it didn't mean anything. But not anymore. Now? It's simple. He loves you. He wants you. He has always wanted you. And the only person who doesn't see it—is you."

I hate to say it. But deep down, I already know she's right.

The final scores are in. Zara takes third, Nina second, and I'm first. The arena erupts with cheers, the sound crashing around me, but it barely registers. People are celebrating. Nina goes back to Drew, his arms already wrapped around her, holding her tight.

But I don't feel like celebrating.

Because Nina's words won't leave my head. Ethan loves me.

I knew it before she said it, but hearing it out loud—hearing it from someone who has seen it, who has felt it, who knows him better than anyone—makes it real in a way I can't ignore.

And I love him.

I've loved him for longer than I've let myself admit.

I knew he was technically still married. I knew Margo was refusing to sign the papers. And still, when things got hard—when he needed me the most—I left. I blocked him. Not because of anything he did, but because I was selfish. Because it was easier to run than to stand beside him and fight.

Nina had every right to blame me. To yell at me. To cut me out of her life.

But she didn't.

She encouraged me. She told me the truth. And now, I can't ignore it.

I look over at the edge of the rink. My parents are there, standing next to Grant and Hannah, all four of them smiling, proud, watching me like I've just accomplished something incredible.

But this isn't the moment that matters.

This isn't the thing that makes my heart race.

Because I already know what I need to do.

I'm done running.

It's time to go home.

It's time to tell Ethan that I love him.

Fourteen
Ethan

I STRAIGHTEN MY TIE, adjusting the knot with a sharp tug. Today is the day. The custody hearing. The moment everything comes to light.

Margo never backed down. She never does. She doesn't want me back. But she wants to win. And she knows the best way to hurt me.

She won't sign the damn papers. Won't let me move on. Won't let go. Instead, she's throwing everything she has at this, using every trick, every lie, every manipulation to take away the one thing that means more to me than anything else.

CC.

I exhale, slow and controlled, gripping the edge of the dresser to steady myself. She's doing this to punish me. Because I rejected her. Because I told her no. Because I wouldn't take her back, no matter how many times she tried.

I wasn't happy with her. I never was. But knowing she hurt our daughter? That was worse than anything else.

Who would've thought that her leaving was the best thing that ever happened to us?

Too bad she didn't stay gone.

"Daddy... why can't I skip school and come?" CC's small voice pulls me from my thoughts. I turn to find her standing in the doorway, her little face pinched in frustration.

I sigh, kneeling so we're at eye level. "Well, sweetheart, this is grown-up stuff."

"But I want to help," she whines, crossing her arms.

I tuck a curl behind her ear, my heart squeezing. She already did. "CC, you did help. You recorded the video for the judge. You told your story. You were so brave." My voice softens, but there's an edge of steel beneath it. "Now it's my turn to protect you."

Her bottom lip wobbles, but she nods. I press a kiss to her forehead, pulling her into a hug.

"Uncle Harold and Aunt Joanne are going to watch you today after school," I continue, forcing a smile. "And Uncle Nikolai is coaching you, along with Aunt Zara."

Her eyes widen, the small spark of excitement cutting through the worry. "Oh! That's exciting!" Then, just as quickly, her face falls. "But... I miss Valeria. Will she be there?"

I freeze.

CC's been asking about her less and less, but it still happens. And every damn time, it hits like a gut punch.

I could lie. I could tell her what I always have—that Valeria is training, that she's busy, that she'll see her soon.

But I don't have that excuse anymore.

So, I tell the truth. The only truth that matters. "I miss her too, squirt."

CC nods, as if she understands something I don't, then skips off. Just like that.

I exhale, dragging a hand down my face. I need to stop thinking about her.

I need to focus. I need to fight.

Because I can't lose CC.

And because Valeria is already gone.

She doesn't want me.

And I have to let her go.

I pull into the courthouse parking lot, gripping the wheel tighter than I need to. This is it. The trial, the fight, the last battle I never wanted but sure as hell won't lose.

I cut the engine and step out, rolling my shoulders, inhaling the cold air like it might settle the tension coiled in my chest. It doesn't.

My parents, Ryan, Nina, and Drew are already on the sidewalk waiting for me. But standing next to Nina is someone I wasn't expecting.

Valeria.

I stop short, my breath locking in my chest. She's here. Not in my memory. Not in my dreams. Right here.

She steps forward, her gaze locked onto mine, steady, unshaken. Determined. "Ethan."

Just my name. Simple. But it slams into me, like something deep and aching finally being touched.

She looks different. But not really. The same, but more.

She's wearing a fitted navy coat, the color making her brown eyes sharper, her skin warmer. It cinches at her waist, elegant, structured, effortlessly her. Her hair is down, waves cascading over her shoulders, the ends curling slightly from the winter air. There's something about it, about all of her, that feels softer. But she's still Valeria. Still steel beneath it all.

Still the woman I love.

I clear my throat, stepping toward her. "You came."

Her lips press together for half a second before she nods. "Of course, I came."

I swallow hard. "You didn't have to."

Her breath shudders slightly, the first crack in her composure. "Yes, I did." She exhales slowly, her breath visible in the cold air. "I left when you needed me. I'm not making that mistake again."

Everything inside me stills.

She left. When things got hard, when Margo came back, when everything was falling apart—she left. And it hurt more than I let myself admit. But now, here she is, standing in front of me, choosing to come back.

Her hands clench slightly, like she's trying to steady herself. "I was scared, Ethan. I was scared of what Margo being back meant, of what it would do to you, to CC. I was scared I would just be in the way." Her throat bobs, her voice barely above a whisper now. "But I wasn't protecting you. I was protecting myself. And that was selfish."

She blinks hard, like she's trying to push past the emotion tightening her voice. "I should've stayed. I should've fought for you. I should've fought for us."

The world around us blurs, the courthouse, the people, the trial waiting inside—none of it exists in this moment. Just her. Just me.

I inhale deeply, letting her words settle, letting them carve into the space where I held my anger, my hurt, my longing for her.

"I understand why you left." My voice is steady, but there's an edge of something else—something real, something raw. "But I also understand why you're here."

She nods, exhaling like she's been holding this in for too long.

"I don't want to be anywhere else."

I reach for her hand, hesitant, waiting for her to pull away.

But she doesn't. Her fingers are cold, but her grip is firm, grounding, sure. She's here. For me. For CC.

I let out a slow breath, squeezing her hand. "Are you sure?"

Her eyes search mine, unwavering. "I love you, Ethan."

The words hit, shatter, and rebuild me within a moment.

I don't realize I've been holding my breath until I let out a quiet exhale. "I love you too."

The tension, the distance, the weeks of uncertainty dissolve between us.

She's here, and she's choosing me. She's choosing us. And I choose her right back.

"What the fuck is she doing here?" Margo's voice slices through the cold air, dripping with the kind of outrage only she can muster.

I turn, already bracing for impact.

Her band stands behind her like a pack of vultures, their smirks smug, arrogant. They think they've already won. They think today will be in their favor. That Callum Hayes, the sleazy attorney she dug up, will rip me apart, tear Valeria down, paint me as the villain.

They have no idea what's coming. They have no idea CC recorded a video, or that Ryan is holding a file thicker than the damn rulebook Margo never followed as a mother. They don't know that we have proof of all the lies she's been spinning, and we'll be turning it all over to the judge.

But they will.

Valeria steps forward, her back straight, her voice calm but steady. Unshaken.

"I'm here for Ethan," she says. "For the Crosse family. For CC."

Margo snaps. "Keep my daughter's name out of your mouth!"

My daughter. Not our daughter. Mine.

Valeria doesn't flinch, doesn't react. She just tilts her head, lips pressing into a thin line.

"You should've thought about your daughter, Margo," she says, voice controlled, cutting. "But you never did."

She turns before Margo can respond, her hand finding mine, her fingers curling around my own like an anchor.

Margo bristles. Livid. Callum steps forward, clearing his throat, his smirk growing. "Well, Ryan," he drawls. "Can't wait for you to explain this one—your client caught in an affair."

Ryan doesn't even blink. Doesn't hesitate. "Sure, Callum. Right after I lay out all of your client's dirty little secrets." He adjusts his tie, all confidence, all control. "Since she wanted to be in front of a judge and all."

Margo scoffs, rolling her eyes. "I have no dirty secrets." Her sneer is almost convincing. Almost. "You're just making things up for Ethan. You've been best friends forever."

Ryan's smirk grows, something lethal beneath it. "Well, the PI says differently."

Silence.

I watch it happen. The way Margo pales, just slightly, her stance shifting, her fingers clenching at her sides. The way Callum stiffens, his smugness flickering, like a man realizing he walked into the wrong fight.

Margo swallows, once, then turns sharply on her heel, storming toward the courthouse steps. Her band follows. Callum follows. They're rattled.

They should be.

I glance at Ryan. "PI?"

He grins, clapping a hand on my shoulder. "You can thank Emilio Blaze for that one. He called in a favor."

I exhale, shaking my head, a quiet pulse of gratitude settling in my chest.

Ryan follows Drew and Nina inside, my parents trailing after them.

I turn to Valeria.

She's watching me carefully. "Are you ready?"

I squeeze her hand, my grip tightening. "As ready as I'll ever be."

We step forward, together. Toward the courthouse. Toward the fight. Toward the ending Margo never saw coming.

Valeria sits with my family, her presence grounding even as I know she hates being here. Emilio and Ana Lucia are near my parents, their expressions unreadable. I square my shoulders, shifting my focus back to the front of the room. Cassidy is at school, safe. That's what matters.

The bailiff steps forward.

"All rise."

The heavy wooden doors open, and the judge enters, taking his seat behind the bench.

"You may be seated."

I grip the table, pulse steadying. Ryan straightens beside me as Margo's attorney, Callum Hayes, rises first. He buttons his expensive suit, stepping forward with calculated ease.

"Your Honor, this is a case of a devoted mother being unjustly alienated from her child. A mother who made sacrifices to support her family, only to return and find herself replaced."

He paces, shaking his head. "We will present evidence that Mr. Crosse engaged in an extramarital affair. That he encouraged his daughter to form an attachment to another woman while pushing her biological mother out. That Mrs. Crosse was forced to fight for a place in her own daughter's life."

Margo shifts, playing the part of the wounded mother, her hands folded neatly in her lap.

Callum delivers his final line smoothly. "We ask this court to restore a mother's rightful place."

Ryan stands. He doesn't button his jacket. Doesn't pace. Just steps forward and speaks. "Your Honor, this is not a case of alienation. It is a case of abandonment."

Margo tenses.

"For eight months, Mrs. Crosse made no attempt to see her daughter. No calls. No visits. No birthday acknowledgment. Not because my client prevented it, but because she chose not to."

Callum shifts in his seat, but Ryan doesn't acknowledge him.

"We will prove that Cassidy Crosse's reluctance to see her mother has nothing to do with manipulation and everything to do with Margo's own actions. We will present evidence—in her own words—that she never wanted this child. That she viewed motherhood as a burden."

Margo exhales sharply, her nails digging into the table.

"This is not about a mother fighting to reclaim her daughter. This is about a mother who left. And now that she sees the life she abandoned moving on without her, she wants control."

He lets the silence settle before delivering his final blow.

"We ask this court to protect Cassidy from further emotional harm. To place her where she is safe. Where she is loved." Ryan returns to his seat.

Silence.

The judge exhales. "Proceed."

Margo rises gracefully, smoothing her skirt as she walks toward the stand. She places her hand on the Bible, voice perfectly composed. "I do."

She sits, crossing her legs neatly. Callum steps forward.

"Mrs. Crosse, why are we here today?"

Margo exhales, looking down as if gathering herself. "Because I want my daughter back."

Her voice trembles just enough to seem real. "Because for months, I have been denied my rights as a mother. Because the man I trusted—the man I built a life with—has taken that away from me."

My jaw locks.

Callum paces. "Can you tell us about your relationship with Cassidy?"

Her face softens. "Cassidy is my world. I gave up so much for her. I put my dreams on hold, because that's what mothers do." She sniffs. "And it breaks my heart that she doesn't know that."

Ryan sits perfectly still.

"Did you have any reason to believe Ethan would cut you out of your daughter's life?" Callum presses.

Margo shakes her head. "No. We had an agreement. He knew this tour was important to me. But when I came back... everything was different." She exhales sharply, shifting forward slightly. "Because I came back to find another woman in my place."

My hands clench into fists under the table.

"I came back to find my husband had moved on. That my daughter had bonded with someone else. That I had been made to feel like I didn't belong in my own family."

She turns, eyes locking onto me with something cold. "Valeria Blaze took everything that was mine."

A murmur ripples through the courtroom.

Callum turns to the judge. "Your Honor, we will prove that Mr. Crosse's relationship with Ms. Blaze directly contributed to the alienation of Cassidy from her mother."

Margo presses a hand to her chest, whispering, "I just want my daughter back."

Callum nods. "Your witness."

Ryan stands, adjusting his cuffs, his expression unreadable. He approaches the stand, resting one hand lightly on the table.

"Mrs. Crosse, at what point did your love for Cassidy include actually being present in her life?"

Margo stiffens. "I have always been there for my daughter."

Ryan lifts a brow. "Really? Because the evidence shows you didn't visit, didn't call, didn't even acknowledge her birthday."

Margo's jaw tightens. "I was on tour."

Ryan doesn't blink. "And in all those months, how many times did you reach out to see her?"

Silence.

Ryan nods. "You claim Cassidy was manipulated into loving Ms. Blaze. But the reality is, she was never given the chance to have a mother who put her first."

Margo shakes her head. "That's not true."

Ryan pulls out a folder. "We have witness testimony—including Cassidy's. Would you like to hear her own words?"

The screen flickers. A trembling voice fills the courtroom. "She doesn't like me."

Margo stiffens.

Ryan doesn't blink. "Mrs. Crosse, do you still believe Ethan is the reason Cassidy doesn't want to see you?"

Silence.

Ryan leans in slightly. "Would you like to hear more?"

Margo looks away.

Ryan smirks. "No further questions."

Callum stands, straightening his suit, preparing for his final attempt to sway the judge.

"Your Honor, what we have here is a clear case of parental alienation. Ethan Crosse not only moved another woman into his daughter's life but actively encouraged Cassidy to see Ms. Blaze as her mother, replacing my client in the process."

He walks to the screen, clicking to display images taken from social media.

"These are public photos of Cassidy attending skating events with Ms. Blaze. This is Cassidy at a family dinner—with Ms. Blaze by her side. And here—" he clicks again, showing a still from Margo's viral video, "—is the moment Mrs. Crosse walked back into her daughter's life, only to find another woman had taken her place."

Margo dabs at her eyes for effect.

Callum presses forward. "We also have proof that Valeria Blaze's presence in Mr. Crosse's life has damaged her reputation—because deep down, even her sponsors saw this for what it is: inappropriate. We have statements from representatives of brands that pulled out of sponsorship deals, citing moral concerns and public backlash."

He turns to the judge.

"Your Honor, what kind of example does this set for Cassidy? A father prioritizing a romantic relationship over his own child? A woman benefiting from scandal? My client simply wants what was stolen from her: her place as Cassidy's mother." Callum sits, smug.

The judge nods. "Mr. Crosse, your response?"

Ryan stands, unbothered, adjusting his tie. He approaches the bench with calm precision, placing a thick folder of documents onto the table. "Your Honor, if we're here to discuss parental alienation, let's talk about the parent who did the alienating—Margo Crosse."

He clicks a remote. Text messages appear on the screen. "These are messages from Margo Crosse to various friends, stating—word for word—her desire to be free of her responsibilities as a mother."

The messages fill the screen:

> "I hope this kid grows up fast so I don't have to deal with her anymore."

> "Ethan can raise her. I didn't ask for this life."

> "She's so needy. I don't have time for that. She's better off with Ethan."

A hush spreads across the courtroom.

Margo shifts in her seat, lips pressing together.

Ryan doesn't stop. "These aren't statements of a devoted mother, Your Honor. These are words from a woman who never wanted to be a mother in the first place."

He clicks again. Financial records appear.

"These documents show that, despite earning a significant income from her music career, Mrs. Crosse has not provided a single financial contribution toward Cassidy's care since she left."

Callum shifts uncomfortably.

Ryan takes a step closer, voice sharp. "She didn't pay for school. She didn't pay for clothes, food, medical expenses. Nothing. In fact, Your Honor, the only thing she's contributed to Cassidy's life in the last eight months—is a lawsuit."

Margo exhales sharply, shaking her head, but Ryan isn't finished.

"And as for my opposing counsel's argument about sponsorship loss? Let's talk about reputation damage."

He presses a button. Screenshots of Margo's affairs flash across the screen. Hotel receipts, messages, photos of her with multiple men—some before she even left for tour.

Gasps ripple through the courtroom.

Ryan turns to the judge.

"Mrs. Crosse didn't leave to chase a dream. She left because she had already checked out of this marriage. And her own words, her own actions, prove she never planned to come back for her daughter."

He lets the silence settle before delivering the final blow. "My client isn't the one who alienated Cassidy from her mother. Margo Crosse did that all on her own."

The judge leans back in his chair, fingers steepled. The weight of everything just presented sits heavy in the room.

After a long pause, he exhales. "I've heard enough."

Margo straightens, eyes widening. Callum leans in, whispering furiously, but she barely hears him.

The judge clears his throat. "This court rules in favor of Ethan Crosse. Full sole legal and physical custody is granted to the father."

Margo stiffens.

"Furthermore, visitation rights are revoked at this time. Before any future considerations, Mrs. Crosse must undergo psychological evaluation and complete extensive parenting courses."

Margo's body snaps upright. "What?" She bolts to her feet, eyes flashing. "You can't do this!"

The judge remains unmoved. "This ruling is final."

Margo's breaths come sharp and fast. Then—she erupts. "You're stealing my daughter!" she screams, whipping toward Ethan. "You did this! You turned her against me!"

Ryan exhales sharply. "No, Margo. You did this to yourself."

Margo turns to the judge. "This isn't fair! I'm her mother!"

The judge doesn't blink. "Then you should have acted like one."

We all rise.

Margo bolts from the courtroom, her heels clicking against the polished floors, her movements sharp, frantic, like she can outrun the reality of what just happened.

She can't.

Callum lingers for a moment, already reaching for his phone, already shifting into damage control. But before he leaves, he turns to Ryan, his expression unreadable.

"I'll get her to sign the papers. Don't worry." He exhales, rubbing his jaw. "Beer later?"

Ryan smirks, shaking his hand. "You got it."

The second the doors open, the second I step into the hallway, my focus zeroes in on the only thing that does matter.

Valeria.

She's standing just ahead, watching me, waiting, her presence grounding me, steadying me, pulling me in like a gravitational force I never had a chance against.

I don't hesitate. I don't think.

I go straight to her, closing the space between us in three strides, and then she's in my arms.

Her breath catches, but she doesn't pull away. She presses into me, solid, real, mine.

I cup her face, tilt her chin up, and kiss her—deep, certain, claiming.

The case is over. Margo is gone. CC is safe.

And now?

Now, it's time to go pick up my girl.

Epilogue
Valeria

THE MUSIC BEGINS, SWELLING through the arena, but I don't hear it the way I used to. I don't count the beats. I don't map out every step before I take it.

I feel it.

I push off, my blades slicing cleanly into the ice. The world outside the rink disappears. The cameras, the judges, the pressure—they all fade away, leaving only the cold air against my skin, the quiet hum of the ice beneath me, and the moment stretching out in front of me.

I start just as I rehearsed. Triple lutz, triple toe. My knees bend, my core tightens, and I launch, rotating fast, sharp, spotting the landing before my blade even touches the ice. Clean. Perfect. Exactly as planned.

But something shifts.

I exhale into my next steps, extending my arms, my fingers reaching, but it feels... wrong. Not because I've made a mistake. But because I've done this before. Every movement, every breath, every single second of this program has been choreographed to be perfect. To win.

But what if winning isn't the point?

The thought stirs, unexpected, curling through my ribs, pressing against something deeper. Do I keep going exactly as planned? Or do I take this moment and make it mine?

For the first time, I hesitate. Just for a heartbeat.

I let go.

The choreography shifts—not enough to break the structure of my program, but enough that it's mine now. A deeper edge here, a longer glide there, a movement I never dared to hold before because it wasn't efficient, wasn't necessary.

I push into my next combination. Triple flip, double toe, double loop. Textbook. But this time, I don't just land it. I absorb the moment, let my arms extend a second longer, let the emotion settle before moving into the next step.

I can hear the crowd reacting.

They feel it.

I push forward, moving into what should be my final jump—a triple loop—but something inside me knows I can do more. Not technically harder. Not riskier. Just more *me*.

So instead of a triple loop, I push into a double axel. The first jump I ever landed. The one that made me fall in love with skating. My blade carves into the ice, and I launch, letting the landing breathe, letting it settle, letting it *mean something*.

I've spent my whole life chasing perfection.

Right now, I just want to skate.

The final spin begins. My body coils in tight, faster, faster, faster—but instead of snapping out as planned, I hold it. The world blurs, the music pulses through my veins, and for the first time, I let it pull me instead of controlling it.

And then, finally, I extend.

Arms reaching. Chin lifting. A finish that isn't just a pose, but a declaration.

The music cuts off.

Silence.

A moment suspended in time. A single breath.

Then—the arena erupts.

Cheers crash through the air, an explosion of sound ricocheting off the walls, the boards, the ice beneath my skates. The crowd is on their feet. The commentators are shouting.

I glide to a stop, my skates pressing against the barrier, my breath coming faster than I want it to. It's over.

The moment I step off the ice, the noise floods back in. The roar of the crowd, the flashing lights, the chaos of movement. It rushes toward me all at once.

I make my way toward Nikolai, where the waiting game begins.

The cameras zoom in, the arena buzzing with restless energy. I wave to the crowd, but my focus is on the scoreboard. The numbers that will decide everything.

My entire career—all the years, the training, the sacrifices—comes down to this.

The arena hushes.

The score flashes onto the board.

230.

Everything inside me stops.

The crowd erupts. Nikolai yells something—something giddy and uncharacteristically proud. But all I can do is stare at the screen.

Gold.

Holy shit, I just won gold.

My knees almost give out. Nikolai grabs me, shaking me in excitement, pulling me into a hug that lifts me off the ground.

"You did it!" he exclaims, gripping my shoulders. "I told you, Valeria!"

I let out a breathless laugh. This is real.

I turn back toward the stands, searching—and I find them immediately.

Ethan is still holding CC, both of them beaming. But CC—she's bouncing, waving something in the air.

A sign.

My name. Big, bold, decorated with glitter and stickers. She's holding it up like she's the proudest kid in the world.

Something in my chest pulls tight.

This is what I've always wanted. A gold medal. A moment like this.

But looking at them—at Ethan, at CC, at the life waiting for me beyond the ice—I realize something.

This isn't the moment that matters most.

They are.

They are my everything.

The podium ceremony is a blur. This is everything I dreamed of.

But for the first time in my life, I know I have more to dream about.

I glance at Ethan one last time, at CC waving her sign.
I have a gold medal.
But more importantly?
I have them.
And what girl wouldn't want that?

Sexy as Sin Series

WELCOME TO THE SEXY AS SIN SERIES, where badass female athletes don't mind working up a good sweat on or off the field.

25 authors. 25 hot stories about fierce female athletes playing hard and finding love.

Bad boys. Good girls. City boys. Country girls. Enemies to lovers. Age gap. One-night stand. Second chances. Sweet and spicy. This collection of sexy novellas will have you cheering from the sidelines.

CHECK OUT THE REST OF THE SEXY AS SIN SERIES HERE!

About the Author

Sara McClaflin, a dedicated author of romance, crafts tales that are not only heart-melting but also delve into the delicate facets of humanity. Having spent the past few years as an avid reader, Sara transitioned from writing book reviews to creating her own narratives. Her passion for romance, in all its diverse forms, shines through as she weaves stories that resonate with readers.

Residing on the vibrant west coast with her husband and beloved dog, Sara McClaflin is surrounded by the inspiration of nature and the love of her family. In her world, there is no such thing as too many books or an overfilled "want to read" list, as each story unfolds new possibilities and adventures.

Newsletter signup: https://sara-mcclaflin.ki t.com/bf24ba8081

a

amazon.com/stores/author/B0CR8VHBHJ/about

ttps://www.instagram.com/authorsaramcclaflin/

facebook.com/profile.php?id=61551822185090

https://twitter.com/authorsaramcc

tiktok.com/@sara.mcclaflin

goodreads.com/author/show/47632250.Sara_McClaflin

Also by Sara McClaflin

Standalone

The Keeper's Secret

The Huntington Brothers Series

Destined for Love

Tangled Hearts

Promises to Keep

Anthologies

Head in the Clouds: A Romantic Comedy Anthology

Desperate: A Deadly Thriller Anthology